NORTHERN GRIZZLIES MC BOOK 9

SILVER'S BULLET

PART OF THE TEMPTED AND TANTALIZING NORTH CAROLINA
REVVED UP ANTHOLOGY
COMPANION TO JANINE INFANTE BOSCO'S
CROSS TO BEAR

INTERNATIONAL BESTSELLING AUTHOR

M. MERIN

Silver's Bullet, Northern Grizzlies MC, Book 9

AI was NOT used in any part of the creation of this book. This, in its entirety, is the sole creation of the author.

This book is intended for adults only. Contains sexual content and language that may offend some. The suggested reading audience is 18 years or older. I consider this book Adult Romance due to language and sexual situations.

Thank you for respecting the hard work of this author.

Published in the United States of America.

Photography: James Critchley Photography

Cover Model: Nathan Smart

Cover Art and Paperback Formatted by Dark Water Covers

Edited: Darlene Tallman

CHARACTERS

Silver – Sam Rawlings, Nomad with NGMC, Idaho chapter

Chains – Cal Fromm, NGMC Idaho. Sophia, his Ol' Lady, and their son, Josh. (NGMC Short Book 1)

Flint – Chairman/previous President of the National Chapter. (NGMC Book 2)

Jasper – current President of the National Chapter. (NGMC Book 1)

NEW CHARACTERS

Vector – President of Roanoke, VA NGMC

Jigsaw – Vector's father, deceased President of VA NGMC

Nadine Morgan – Jigsaw's Old Lady. Mother of Satan's Knights, Maverick and Shady by Preacher.

Bridget Morgan – Jigsaw and Nadine's daughter.

Members of NGMC Virginia Chapter: Roman, Oak, and Piercer

Maggie Dennison – camera operator, Silver's love interest

Fred Dennison – Maggie's grandfather

Diane Dennison – Maggie's grandmother

Nathan Rawlings – Silver's brother

Alex Rawlings – Nathan's daughter with his ex-girlfriend

Michael Rawlings – Nathan and Silver's father, deceased

Prim – Nathan's ex and Alex's mom

Di – Vlogger, Maggie's boss

Carter – retired sheriff

Tusco – current sheriff

Anyone referred to as a Satan's Knight can be found in Janine Infante Bosco's works.

PROLOGUE

SILVER

SUMMER OF 2023, IN IDAHO

"I'm just saying, this is a man who doesn't want to be found," Wrench verbalizes the obvious. "The guy's been a ghost, until last week when some vlogger posted this story."

"Come again?" I ask, never hearing the word *vlogger* before.

"A self-appointed social media journalist whose medium is short videos," Riley interjects, immediately understanding the word that threw me off.

"If this guy is your brother, and I can definitely see some similarities between you, he caught the vlogger's attention and she turned into a pit bull trying to find out more about him," Wrench says before turning and tapping the monitor in front of him.

"Well, it wasn't easy, loyal viewers, but I believe I'm standing outside the gate that guards the property of the man I've been referring to as Justice," a woman with long purple and blue hair stands, nearly bouncing with excitement, outside a gate that has a big sign attached to it. The camera zooms in on that while the vlogger continues speaking.

Absolutely NO Trespassing.

I don't want to buy anything from you.

I don't care about your religious views.

You wouldn't be standing there reading this if I had invited you,

so you will be shot and fed to my hogs if you take another step.

"Di, we should get going," another woman's voice says from behind the camera and the focus suddenly shifts from the sign to the woods beyond the gate. "I think we're being watched."

"There," the vlogger, who's ironically called Di and may indeed be about to, points to the woods. "Excuse me! I see you removed the note I taped to your fence. Can we talk? Is this a good time, Mr. Rawlings?"

Just as my hands form into fists at the sound of my

last name, we all hear the very distinct sound of someone pumping a shotgun and the camera woman starts to back away.

"Maggie, get back here. He's not actually going to shoot us," Di says insistently, showing us who the brains of this operation is.

Hint: it isn't the vlogger.

She lets out a sigh before she continues. "Alright, loyal viewers, my sidekick is hiding behind her Jeep, so I hope you are at least getting a great view of the scenery. As you know, I've been on the trail of that *hot hunk of Avenger-like* man, since we all saw the clips of him saving those women in Asheboro last week. It's not often something of that magnitude falls into my own backyard, and we all know I have the knack for cutting through the bull and finding the true story.

"Yes, my competitors focused on the human-trafficking aspect of it, but what is the story behind our hero? And what conspiracy is in the works, that the mystery man is no longer being mentioned?" Di seems to hear something behind her, and suddenly grips her microphone with both hands. "As best as I can tell, this might very well be his property and if so, his name is Michael Rawlings and get this, ladies, I couldn't find a marriage license for him on record in the area."

Just then something flies at the vlogger's head and screams are issued from both women as something white hits the vlogger's colorful hair and bounces harmlessly off. The camera shifts to where Di leans down to pick it up and it's clearly a balled-up piece of paper.

"You did get my letter! Here, hold onto it, all of my contact deets are on it," Di says, trying to slide the smoothed-out sheet in between the planks of the sign.

The camera pans wide again before Di waves so her cohort will focus on her for her sign-off and a tease about a future episode of this shitshow, but that's when Wrench reverses the footage and blows up an image in the background. The lighting is piss-poor which leads to Wrench's previous point, it could easily be me standing there in the shadows.

"What did she mean, about him saving some people?" I needlessly ask him. He grins at me and points to Riley who has other footage ready to roll.

This time, a reporter from a legitimate news source talks about a good Samaritan who comes out of nowhere, saving two college aged girls who had been drugged and taken from a bar. Choppy footage, pieced together from area cameras show him fighting off three men, leaving them shattered on the ground. The clearest part of the rescue is when he sits the girls up against a wall and stands over them, while making a call on a cell phone that he picked up off the ground. When he disconnects the call, he places the phone beside one of the girls and pulls his shirt off to wrap around his arm, which is clearly bleeding; waiting until the cops and paramedics arrive to take over the scene.

At some point after that, he seems to disappear in the middle of the confusion and the reporter asks the public for help in identifying the *hero*.

"Since Michael was your father's name, I'm guessing the property is in his name, but the man in the video looks and moves like you, so he could easily be Nathan," Wrench concludes, looking between Jasper and me.

"Excuse me a second," Riley says quietly, getting up to leave the room like she always does when she senses club discussions coming on.

"I'll let Vector know you'll be out his way," Jasper says, mentioning the president of the furthest east Northern Grizzlies chapter. "If your brother is in North Carolina, then Virginia should be an easy ride from there."

"Jasper, all the resources you've afforded me over the years, there's no way I can ever repay you," I tell him, before reaching an extended hand to Wrench. "Or you, brother. And if this doesn't pan out, I'm done looking. I can't dedicate my entire life to searching for someone who has forgotten about me."

"I'd have done the same, even for another hour with my own brother, Silver," Jasper quietly responds, shaking my hand after Wrench does.

"Unless you need me for anything around here, I'll

spend tonight out at Chains and Sophia's, then head out tomorrow."

"I'll message you everything I have, including contact information for that vlogger," Wrench says, cracking a grin at that last shot. That stops me in my tracks for a moment.

"Any idea who that Maggie woman is? I prefer someone with a deeper sense of self-preservation," I ask him on the outside chance he knows anything.

"Makes me wonder how you ever get laid, if that's your preference..." Jasper cracks, getting a bark of laughter from Wrench.

"On the road again," I burst out into song as I leave them, eager to share the news with Chains.

After playing the videos over for Chains that night, he gets as excited as I am—knowing how long I've been trying to find the brother I only have the faintest memories of, from my early years.

ONE

SILVER

SUMMER OF 2024

It's unreal, how much your life can change in a year's time.

Last summer, I rode across the country to find a brother I hadn't seen since I was five or six. The first meeting was a little dicey, which is one way of saying I ended up catching some buckshot in my arm. Nathan later blamed me, saying I didn't duck fast enough.

It was almost immediately after that, when he took a closer look at me and asked my name, that I saw any trace of the boy that I remembered.

The last time I had seen him, he was staring out the

back window of our father's car, silently crying as he was driven away. Our parents announced that they were divorcing and that we would be spending six months with each parent, then switching. The most obvious flaw with their plan being that Nathan and I would not be raised together. I'll never understand the logic behind that, but the next trade off never happened and later that year, my mom signed me off to foster care.

We'll never know the truth of what actually went down, but our father had told Nathan that Mom and I had been killed in a car accident. Further questions went unanswered, until he finally stopped asking.

I quickly came to understand that my brother lives in the here-and-now. He wasn't interested in talking about what it was like growing up with our old man, so I respected his boundaries. Mainly, we took to hunting together and later, spending time with his daughter, Alex.

It was a solid month after we were reunited that I even found out that I was an uncle. While Nathan didn't seem to mind my presence in his home from time-to-time, I didn't want to push my luck, so I let Vector know that I'd be available to help his chapter out with the odd runs and jobs whenever needed.

Flint had warned me that the Virginia Northern Grizzlies were a tight knit crew, but that was barely the half of it. I had stayed with them on previous occasions, however, visiting and living with them were completely different animals.

Vector had been in the Army, and while he always seemed calm and deliberate on the outside, it was like there was a beast rumbling under his skin—just waiting for its moment to be set free. He never talked about the six years he was away, and not even his closest friends, Roman and Oak, knew the story behind his limp.

The most startling difference between our chapter and theirs was Bridget. Vector's half-sister had been raised at the clubhouse, and after spending her college years away, she came back with a finance degree and a plan to launder money.

I didn't really know anything about her until I stowed some of my shit in a room at their clubhouse and was put on the payroll. Since then, it's become apparent that Jasper trusts her enough to have her helping him with their accounts also.

Most of what I know about Bridget came from comments the other brothers have made, more than anything she directly told me, but she's a hellcat—in the best meaning of the term.

Once, deep in a bottle of gin, Vector told me about the night her mother showed up, uncertain of her welcome. It was members only in the clubhouse that night when in she walked, Nadine's hand resting on the curve of her belly and without a word she stopped in the center of the room. His father, Jigsaw, looked up from his card game long enough to claim her as his Ol' Lady.

In the coming months, they were at war with the Knights and even with blood shed on both sides, Jigsaw never wavered. It was the night that the president of the Knights got a few bullets into him that his Ol' Lady saw the choice she had to make. She could look to the future or live in the past. Nadine was truly his other half and she remained by his side until his death nearly fifteen years after that day.

Bridget reminds me of my niece in some ways, and I smile at the thought of meeting that kid for the first time. Not long after my brother and I had been reunited, I took a chance and rode out from the clubhouse, eager to spend more time getting to know Nathan and run a half-baked idea past him. Using my key to unlock his gate, I was securing it behind me when I heard the sound of his shotgun being loaded.

By then, I thought we were past that stage, so turning in the direction of the sound my face quickly shifted from my *what the hell?* expression to my *what the fuck?* expression when I saw a slip of a girl lining me up in her sights.

"Who the hell are you?" we both asked at the same time.

Normally I would stand taller, trying to intimidate

her, but having felt the bite of Nathan's homemade shells before, I decided to play it safe.

"I'm Nathan's brother, Sam," I told her.

"He doesn't have a brother, asshole," she growled, in a pretty fair imitation of Nathan.

"He thought I was dead and he wasn't an easy guy to track down," I explained the situation, all the while studying her for some trace of who she was. "Plus, he gave me a key."

At that point, her head was cocked to the side, her lips were sealed together in a straight line, and her eyebrows were touching as she processed the information. It was her russet-colored hair that threw me off for a moment, but she was undoubtably related to him.

"Are you his sister or his daughter?" I asked the girl who has barely reached her teenage years.

"Alex, I'd rather you didn't shoot him," my brother's voice called from the woods and the gun was immediately lowered. "I was going to tell you about him tonight. Sam, my daughter Alex, unexpectedly showed up yesterday."

I removed the bandana from my head, wiping the sweat from my hands before extending one to her.

"Well, you could have just done that to start with," she said, rolling her eyes before they landed on the silver swatch of hair that her father and I have in common.

"I'm an uncle, huh?" I needlessly asked, sporting a

large smile as I looked between them. "That's pretty fucking cool."

"Please don't say I have to call him Uncle Sam," she said, trying not to laugh when she looked at her dad and popped the shell out, before returning his shotgun. "That's so cheesy."

"You make a solid point," Nathan replied, grinning over her shoulder at me. "He prefers Silver anyway."

Later that night, after Alex had crashed, Nathan opened up with me about the volatile relationship he had been in for years. He finally called it quits when Alex was eight and had been fighting for more and more custody ever since.

Alex's mom had started dating some guy who came through town from time to time, and when his ex would take off with him, his daughter would randomly show up on his doorstep. The only part of that he minded, was having to keep a lawyer and the county informed of the unplanned visits, since he had spent his life staying off the grid.

"Well, this might mix up a thought I had, but here's why I came out here today." I hem and haw a bit about the idea that had been forming in my mind. "I've told you about Chains and how we always spend Christmas together. I was going to try to get you to come back with me, to meet all the guys and his Ol' Lady."

"I appreciate that, and spending time with you." He

stopped talking, sitting back in his chair. I knew him well enough to understand that he was chewing on what I said, so I gave him a few minutes to get his thoughts together. "I don't feel right leaving Alex with how her mom's acting nowadays, but do you think Chains and Sophia would consider coming out here? I know it's a hard time of year to travel and she has a service dog and their son, but they could have my bedroom. If you help me, we can get that shack out back into shape. You and me sleep out there, leaving Alex free to sleep in her room when, and if, she's here."

I unconsciously placed my hand over my heart, scratching at my skin as the organ felt like it was outgrowing the cavern it beat in. "I'll ask them."

"Wanna beer?"

"Fuck yeah." The words escaped with my breath, and I nodded when he quickly returned with one for each of us. "Thank you."

He clinked his bottle against mine, knowing that it wasn't the beer that I was thanking him for.

The memories of that day run slowly through my mind as I stare down at the urn in my hands, once again grateful to have my Brothers at my back.

PART ONE

STARTING IN THE SUMMER OF 2023

TWO

MAGGIE

NORTH CAROLINA

She's so fucking annoying, I think for the zillionth time as I gauge the lighting near the fence leading onto the Rawlings property. I had pleaded with her to make it out here earlier today, but the hair tutorial that she wanted to try out went hysterically wrong, forcing her to wash her hair and start over. Unfortunately, I wasn't filming that.

Di and I went to school together but ran in very different circles. As she's chased her ambitions to become an influencer, I've been building my photography and graphic design business. It's just my bad luck that Di's the best paying gig I've had, so I smile and nod along with her cockamamie ideas. At least I will until her dad gets tired of funding this, or she actually blows up and dumps me for a film crew with more experience.

I'm not under any illusion that loyalty is part of our deal.

"I'm ready to get started," Di announces, snapping her fingers. "Hey, you're still available to go into the city with me this weekend, right? I think I can get some unique human-interest stories, then you can do your edits to put together a few two-minute clips."

"Maybe if we're really lucky, we'll witness a carjacking," I deadpan, keeping a straight face as I make one last adjustment to the light diffuser I set up near her. Does she even hear herself? A two-minute clip for a human-interest story? I wonder if I get points for not replying, *those should be insightful and deep*.

"That would be amazeballs, but only if you were ready to film. Didn't you want to get this done before we lost the light?" she answers back in her sugary-sweet voice, like I'm the reason for the late start.

As soon as I begin filming a light hits my camera, and I have to signal for her to start over as I change my position. This time, someone's pointing a laser at her face—there's a red dot that's moving in a circle.

"Knock it off!" I call out, looking behind me to try to get a glimpse of whoever is messing around.

"What's going on?" she asks me, looking confused.

"Your mystery man is acting like a ten-year-old," I yell out, louder than I need to and almost immediately feel something hit the back of my head. "Asshole!"

Di yells something in annoyance as I'm spinning around, there's a Nerf bullet on the ground at my feet and I look up to see Di get nailed in the middle of her forehead. Since there's no way the man crossed the road with us standing here, there are two of them and they were waiting for us.

"Did you say anything about coming out here again?" I call out to her as I open the door of my Jeep for some cover.

"Of course, I did. My viewers have been asking, so I did a teaser about following up today," she answers me, wedging herself between me and the driver's seat. "Look, I'm hosting a party tonight, I don't have time to wait them out. Let's just go."

"I can't leave my equipment," I explain, getting an overly dramatic roll of her eyes in response as we continue to get pummeled. "Help me break it down real fast and we can get out of here."

Keeping my head down, I start for my camera stand. Di makes it about two steps before calling out in frustration again. "You know what, it's your equipment. I'll call you tomorrow about the trip."

With that, she hightails it to her BMW and takes off. I'm not even going to pretend to be surprised, what does surprise me is that a whistle rings out the moment she's gone, and it seems to be the signal for a ceasefire.

"Thank you!" I call out, more than a little pleased that they didn't seem to target my equipment. If anything had been damaged, I'd be out money I don't have.

"Need some help?"

I spin around at the sound of a deep, rough voice. Cocking my head to the side, I study the man on the other side of the gate, from his heavy black boots, up to the shock of silver in an otherwise full head of black hair.

"You're younger than I thought you'd be, Nathan," I tell him after a moment. "And no, I'd rather you didn't mess with my equipment."

"Your vlogger friend used the name, Michael. How do you know about Nathan?" The momentarily surprised expression on his face is quickly replaced with curiosity as he unlocks the gate.

"My *employer,*" I stress the word, so he doesn't lump her into my friend category. "Can't be bothered to *investigate* anything beyond running a quick search online. I spent ten minutes in the diner with old Barnie Thompson and he told me all about you, your dad, and your daughter—who I sincerely hope is out of ammo because she's one hell of a shot."

"Thank you!" A girl's voice rings out behind me,

and the man and I share a grin as she remains out of sight.

"Well, you did better than your fri… employer, but I'm not Nathan," he tells me, bending over to pick up some of the yellow and blue Styrofoam bullets. "I'm not sure I've been added to the gossip mill yet. I'm Silver, Nathan's long-lost brother."

My eyes widen with his words, not having heard any of this scuttlebutt. I pause for a moment, trying to decide if I should hit the record button on the camera but decide to leave him his privacy. "Oh boy! I bet information like that would get me free pancakes at the diner!"

He chuckles as I carefully pack up my camera and cross to pack up the diffuser.

"And you're Maggie," he says with a grin on his face. "I was hoping we'd cross paths, so when my niece told me Di posted something about coming by today, we set our trap."

"Some good old-fashioned bonding, huh?"

"Well, I don't have much experience babysitting, so Nathan's getting what he paid for," he drawls out, and I realize that for better or worse, we have a similar sense of humor.

We chat as I slowly pack my things and get them situated in the back of my Jeep as he goes about using the excuse of collecting the Nerf ammo to check me out.

"Why do you work for her?" he asks me suddenly.

"Because I need the money, and since I get video credits, it's helping to build my resume," I tell him honestly. "It's just that she told me very early on that the, and I quote, 'the only thing I needed to think about was filming her and getting the best angles'. So now, even if I know more about a topic that she's talking about, I keep it to myself."

"Is she your main client then?" he asks.

"No, I do wedding and family photography. If I cover parades and church events, the local papers will occasionally buy some of my images, and I dabble in graphic design, but that's a lot of one-off jobs around here, so it doesn't pay great."

He nods to himself, putting the last of the bullets into the bag that he has hooked up to his belt before he speaks again. "What about book covers?"

"What do you mean?" I ask, momentarily startled when I see how close he's standing to me all of sudden.

"My friend's Ol' Lady," he says, and my eyes widen at the term before shifting back down to his cut that he's wearing. "She writes and self-publishes her own books, so she outsources that kind of stuff. Why don't you give me your number and website info so I can pass it on to her?"

I cock my head to the side, suddenly having dozens of questions about motorcycle clubs, but I bite my bottom lip as I try to read his intent. "Is that a roundabout way of getting my number for yourself?"

"It can be anything you want it to be." His smile has taken on a wolfish quality as he takes another step forward so we're practically toe-to-toe.

I'd like to think that the way he was looking at my lips meant he would have kissed me, right here on the side of the road. Unfortunately, his niece started making retching noises.

"Brat," he growls, looking past my shoulder to the woods on the other side of the road. He hands me his phone and I quickly dial my number from it.

"I'll text you my website when I get home. I'd be interested in talking to your friend, even if you don't use my number yourself," I tell him, long ago learning that it's important to ask for a job that you want, even while I cringe at my lame attempt at flirting.

"Her name's Sophia. Service is spotty out here, but I will text her. And you," he assures me.

"You can kiss her now, I'm not looking!" the girl calls out and I take a step back as he takes one forward.

"Does she have any more ammo for her Nerf gun?" I ask him. Immediately having put myself in her shoes, I know if I had a chance to have fired at any of my friends who were kissing when we were younger, I would have nailed them.

"Oh!" He narrows his eyes when my words register before slowly nodding. "Excellent point. Though I don't know if I like it that you might be as diabolical as she is."

"That just means I'll never be boring," I sass back, finally getting behind the wheel and closing the door. I give him what I hope is a cute smile before I start the engine and change the gear. "Bye now."

"Bye for now," he calls in reply.

My more controlled grin shifts into a huge dorky smile and I blast the '80's station, enjoying the oldies, and the possibility of hanging out with Silver. If I had to guess, he's probably eight to ten years older than me and while he's what's considered traditionally hot, it's more his personality that's right up my alley.

I've lived in Yanceyville nearly ten years and I know all the guys within my age range. Silver might be a smidge older than me, but considering that the dating pool in this town is comprised of people living within a mile of their exes, I am more than delighted to have a crack at someone new.

THREE

SILVER

The sound of my bike cuts through the peaceful neighborhood and following Maggie's very careful directions, I bypass the red brick house and cut up the driveway to the well-built garage, smiling when she opens the door next to the large garage door.

Striding toward me, she's acting more like I'm a getaway vehicle rather than a date, when the backdoor to the main house opens and an older lady leans out, smiling and waving at me in greeting.

"Gram, no," Maggie moans, stopping dead in her tracks and looking defeated.

I turn off my bike and throw a wink in the older woman's direction. "Maggie, if I'd known your grandmother was home, I'd have brought her flowers."

"Oh, Maggie, he's a hunky one. Invite him in to meet your grandfather," the gray-haired woman says insistently, motioning us with one hand as she turns to call out to, I assume, her husband.

"You don't have to do this," Maggie whispers, her cheeks having turned scarlet. "She can be… a lot."

"And here I thought you were excited to see me, instead you wanted to keep me a secret," I tease her as I slowly stalk toward her. "But first."

Slowly leaning down, I give her the chance to duck away from me, but she catches my intent and leans up to meet my lips half-way. My hand cups her check, feeling the heat from her blush and I chuckle, thinking of her grandmother's words, before I deepen our kiss, enjoying the taste of her.

Too soon, she pulls back from me. "We'd better get in there or she'll come out looking."

"Just been wanting to do that since the other day," I tell her, sliding my hand down along the front of her body, promising myself I'll explore it later, but for now, I settle for intertwining my hand in hers.

I let her lead the way inside the kitchen and grin when I see her grandmother fanning herself with a dishtowel. The man sitting at the table shares a fond smile with Maggie.

"I tried to get her moving earlier, but I swear she knew we were up to something," he says before looking at me. "Fred Dennison, this is my wife, Diane."

"Nice to meet you, sir," I reply, then dusting off manners that Chains' uncle taught me long ago, I hold out my hand to shake his. "I'm Sam Rawlings. Diane, thank you for your warm welcome."

"Don't be daft," she says, laughing as she puts a plate of cookies on the square formica table and motions for me to sit. "It was Maggie who gave you the *warm* welcome. We are happy to meet the reason she's been smiling like a loon lately, though."

"Oh, has she?" I ask, turning to grin at the loon in question—and very happy she's not armed, before reaching for a cookie. "I have to tell you, I've been just as excited for our date."

"What are your plans tonight?" Diane asks me, crossing back and forth to the fridge as she pours out four glasses of milk without asking anyone if they actually want it.

"We're going to go for a ride, then grab a bite, I guess," I almost fumble the response, not really having had anything in mind other than hoping for third base. I look over to where Maggie has seated herself to my left and raise an eyebrow, looking for some help.

"Do tell," she nearly purrs, and I read the dare in her eyes as I take a bite out of the cookie. "What were you thinking for dinner?"

I start choking on the crumbs in my throat, remembering the rather explicit conversation we had the other night. Somehow, I don't think Fred wants to hear what I promised to feed his granddaughter.

"Oh! I know! Why don't you come to Bingo night with us!" Diane exclaims, looking thoroughly excited as she dips her cookie in her glass of milk.

Just before Maggie squeezes her eyes tightly closed, I swear I see her pinch herself. Fred starts coughing, mainly to cover the chuckle that had come out originally.

"Gram, no," Maggie repeats what she said earlier. "It's our first date."

"Your grandmother and I met at the church Bingo. Back when the dinosaurs roamed the land and kids were expected to spend time with their parents," Fred interjects. "However, on a night like this and with a bike like what's parked in the driveway, I think Maggie would prefer Sam's plan."

"Don't you listen to him, Sam," Diane replies, her eyes imploring me to take her side before she continues in the worst stage whisper I've ever heard. "Besides, the first time Fred ever got laid was during Bingo!"

"Gram! No!" Maggie claps her hands over her ears and tucks her head down as she screeches out what's fast becoming a litany.

My head is spinning at the amount of crazy that continues to fall out of Diane's mouth, but I'm having too much fun, so I grab another cookie. "Do they serve food there, or should we grab something before we go?"

"I made sandwiches for us already, but I'll throw together two more for you and Maggie," Diane says, clapping her hands together in excitement. "Mags, gather up whatever snacks and drinks you and this strapping man want and add them to our cooler."

Resigned, Maggie stands up, briefly stopping to whisper in my ear. "I will bide my time, but there will be payback for this."

When she's reaching up to grab a bag of chips from a cabinet, I let out a low whistle. "I forgot to tell you that you look beautiful."

Maggie's glare has softened when she looks over her shoulder.

"Thank you," Diane answers.

"He meant Maggie," Fred sounds as frustrated as Maggie looks at Diane's response. "Sam, I'd like to assure you, my wife isn't crazy."

"I wasn't, but fifty years with this man..." Diane claps back.

"Fred, what do I need to know about Bingo?" I ask him.

"We're out of beer!" Maggie calls out.

"Oh, God. And we're going to need it tonight. Diane, finish those sandwiches, we're going to buy a case on the way to the church hall!" Fred stands up, talking and moving faster than he has since I walked in.

"Wait, we can bring beer to your church?"

"Bingo is BYOB," Fred answers, clapping me on the shoulder before helping Diane put the extra food in the fanciest cooler I've ever seen. "Do you want to ride with us? There's room in the SUV."

I look at Maggie and she shrugs. "In for a dollar..." she says. Maybe it's just watching her squirm that has me looking forward to what's bound to be a BYOB Bingo shitstorm, but I'm starting to get the feeling that Maggie and I aren't going to be a casual thing.

Even though Fred pretends to put up a fight, he allows me to buy the case of beer and doesn't say a word when I pop a can open in the back seat.

After I take a couple of swigs, Maggie reaches out for it and helps herself to a long, deep swallow, giving me a wink when she returns the empty can. "We're here."

And sure enough, Fred is turning into a large parking lot. "The church is two blocks away from their house, but they drive due to the cooler," she explains. "Granted the liquor store is a little further away."

Before tonight, I would never have considered bingo a competitive sport, but my mind is quickly and forever changed when I grasp the sheer volume of cards being sold, not to mention all the extras. We get settled in, Maggie, Fred, and I holding the table while enjoying the beer. Meanwhile, Diane makes her way around to all the other tables to chat with everyone before the game gets started.

The topic of conversation is no mystery. Maggie's face is as red as a berry and any time I look over to Diane, she's motioning to me in some manner.

"How did you two meet?" Fred asks, looking between us.

"He and his niece ambushed me. It was brutal, I almost didn't survive," Maggie replies with a smirk on her face.

"Guilty. Although in my defense, we were only armed with Nerf guns."

"Maggie was probably sore someone got the drop on her," Fred chuckles. "Her practical jokes are legendary."

I raise an eyebrow at the woman before me, her chin is tilted up and her expression is filled with pride at his words. Once again, I see that spark in her eyes that tells me I'll have my hands full with her every step of our journey.

"Do tell." I lean down to pull a few more beers out of the cooler, offering them to my hosts.

"I think it's best if you find out for yourself," Fred responds, clinking his bottle against mine.

Over the next couple of hours, I win two rounds of bingo and Maggie wins another. Throughout the evening I watch the three Dennisons, and wonder more and more about how the older couple came to raise her. The relationship they demonstrate is undoubtedly special, but they never once treat her as a child; not in the ways I've seen other family units do, as they struggle with watching a juvenile grow into adulthood.

"You better get him out of here soon, Maggie," Fred whispers after looking at the nine cards in front of me. "There'll be a riot if he wins again."

"BINGO!" Maggie shrieks out, and I notice the voices around us are, indeed, sounding less congenial.

"Time to go, babe," I whisper into her ear when I lean over to kiss her for her win. "Fred, do you want me to put your cooler in your SUV before I head out?"

"No, someone always offers," he responds when Maggie goes up to collect her prize.

"You're welcome to join us again, Sam," Diane tells me, keeping her voice low. "Just maybe give it a couple of weeks."

After I kiss Diane's temple, I turn to her husband.

"Your father was a tortured soul, Sam," Fred says, using our clasped hands to pull me close to him. "You might want answers for what happened, but as an old man looking in, I'd advise you to count your blessings. Nathan's childhood was not an easy one."

At this moment, looking into Fred's wise but wary eyes, my heart slows for just a second before it leaps into double-time.

He's right. I have Nathan and Alex now. That's enough.

Somehow, I think if I pressed for information, he'd tell me more than I'd even want to know but chasing ghosts never did anyone any good. As I watch Maggie returning from collecting her price, I know the smile that splits my face doesn't escape the old man's notice.

She smiles and nods at people, but deftly avoids any attempts to draw her into conversation. When her gaze lands on me, I know what she's thinking and I'm eager to comply.

"Be good to her."

I look down at Fred, giving him a slow deliberate nod. It's more of a promise, really.

"All set," Maggie says when she stops beside us, waving the thirty bucks at her face like it's a fan. She admonishes her grandparents to keep up our streak and tilts her head toward the door.

MAGGIE

"And now reporting from outside the church hall, how does the big winner feel about his debut performance?" I ask Silver, imitating Di's voice to a T and holding an invisible microphone obnoxiously in front of his face.

"I don't know, what are the chances of me being the *big winner* tonight?" He laughs at my nonsense, using my fisted hand to pull me into his arms, and spinning us around. I can't help the laugh that wells up out of me, nor the smile that remains when he tucks me into his side, his arm around my shoulders, as we hurriedly walk back to my place.

"We're not having sex tonight," I inform him, wanting to get that out of the way. "But I'd like it if you came up."

"Messing around with you, in any way, shape, or form, makes me the big winner, Maggie," he replies, and the sincerity in his voice takes the cheesy edge off his words.

"You're so full of shit," I snort, not sure of where this is going. I walk faster but reach for his hand to tug him along. "Hurry up, it's chilly."

"Um, I have a couple of beers in the fridge…" That's as far as I get after I unlock the door leading into my place above my grandparents' garage.

Silver pulls me back, and his mouth quickly lands on mine, his hands slide down my sides to cup my ass cheeks and he pulls me up. I wrap my legs around his hips, but break off the kiss just long enough to point toward the small room beyond the kitchenette. "There."

His long strides eat up the meager distance and even though he'd barely stopped kissing me he doesn't have any problem finding his way to my bed; I hold him tighter when I feel him sitting down. When Silver tugs my shirt up over my head, I open my eyes a smidge to confirm that I'd cleared away all the clothes earlier. The closet door gave up its struggle against the pile I had shoved in there and is cracked open, but the feel of his tongue on my nipple wipes that worry from my mind.

I moan, reaching down to push my breasts up and enjoy the feel of his mouth moving back and forth between them. Shifting my hips forward, I know I want a taste of the hardness I feel inside of his jeans, so I reach for his buckle.

"No sex tonight," he says, reminding me of my earlier words as he swats my hand away.

"But I just want to…"

"You take my jeans off, there's no way I'm not fucking you." His words are firm and instead of splashing ice water over me, incite a fire in my veins like I've never felt before.

"What if I just want a taste?" I ask, gripping his belt buckle. My indecision must have been written all over my face because he tugs my hand away to bring it up to his lips.

"No sex tonight. Now, take your pants off and lay down," he says, startling me with the contradiction, before he continues with a wink. "I aim to leave a good impression."

The look he's giving me leaves little doubt as to what's in store, so I hurry to comply and am relieved I always take the time to maintain a clean slate down there. When I'm spread out before him, I squirm at his perusal until I see the look in his eyes.

There's not a doubt in my mind that he *really* likes what he's so intently studying. I'm nervously twisting my hands together over my ribcage and when he notices, he leans toward them blowing a raspberry on the skin just below them.

Some random noise between a scream and a laugh bursts from my throat as my knees jerk up. "Silver!"

Instead of saying anything, he settles in between my thighs and just as he threads one of his large, calloused hands through both of mine, I feel his tongue on my lower lips, tentatively mapping out the terrain.

I shift my knees up and press his hand flat against my stomach as I methodically stroke the top of it. The heel of his hand presses down on all the butterflies fluttering in my pelvic region, just as his tongue finds my clit. With the lightest pinch of his teeth around the sensitive bud, I moan, enjoying the pressure around my clit as he rhythmically strokes it with his tongue.

His other hand is busy, his middle finger swiping through my folds and into my core. I squeeze down tightly when I register the intrusion. It's the growl he lets out, vibrating against me that nearly sends me over the edge.

Silver shifts up to kiss me, using his fingers to make sure I come. I don't know if it's a mixture of my juices on his tongue, or the intensity that's rolling off of him, but I grab his wrist and swing my leg over his hip — so desperate to finish that I use his hand as proxy for my own.

"Oh," I sigh, leaning my head against his chest.

"Are you a, I mean, have you… before?" he asks, and I look up at him, wondering at the startled expression on his face. "Sex, Maggie, not just getting off."

I shrug and his nostrils flare with frustration.

"Almost, but not really, I guess," I hedge. "It didn't really feel like he did, but afterwards he told everyone we did it. Why?"

"Tell me you dumped his sorry-one-pump ass?" Silver responds, kissing my forehead. "Babe, you're still a virgin."

"And you're a, what? A gynecologist, when you aren't crossing the country on your sexy beast of a bike?" I ask, upset at his line of questioning. Pissed off that I even answered him, I sit up to look for my T-shirt.

"I felt your fucking hymen," Silver responds, sounding angrier than I am. "Christ, how old are you?"

"Nineteen," I mumble, trying to hold back my tears. My head is spinning between how he made me feel and his news—which obviously has pissed him off.

I barely have my shirt on before his arm wraps around my waist and he pulls me back against his body.

"Mags, you wanna know how old I am?" he whispers the question into my ear.

"I know you're older than me, what does it matter?" I spit back, keeping my spine rigid in an attempt to ice him out.

He lets out a long breath before shifting onto his back, keeping me firmly by his side. "I can't promise you anything, Mags. I don't live here, not anywhere really."

When he pauses, I decide to pick up the slack. "Should have figured you were too old for me."

With that he lifts his head to raise an eyebrow at me, the question clear in his eyes.

"You agreed to play fucking Bingo. With. My. Grandparents," I nearly screech, twisting even closer to him and flicking his chest. "I wanted to go for a ride and then, y'know, mess around."

He starts laughing and I can't help but to join him, glad he can take a hit without getting huffy.

"I'm pegging you for thirty," I say, throwing out a rough estimate that's mainly based on what I learned about his brother.

"Add a few years to that," he answers me and honestly, it's better than I thought.

"I'll be twenty soon," I offer.

"I'm still trying to figure out why Fred didn't chase me off with a shotgun," he answers, sounding like he's in pain.

"Ha, please. My grandma's like ten years older than him. He was dating her sister, then they hooked up and had to move up here from Georgia because of the scandal."

"Granny for the win!" Silver chuckles, sounding impressed.

"You don't need to stick around," I say, offering him an out, but crazy-happy when he blows off my question and finally kicks off his boots, before he pulls my comforter over us.

It's nice, after years of being in this bed alone and wondering when I would be able to escape this town to meet a man who didn't know everything about me, to be able to share my past and hear about Silver's.

FOUR

MAGGIE

"What happened to your parents?" he asks me close to dawn.

His voice sounds both hesitant yet curious and I weigh my words, trying to decide how much I want to tell him.

"That too deep for tonight?" he asks, and I roll into his body again, pressing my lips against his throat. I nearly groan, smelling myself on the scruff lining his jaw. Who knew that'd be such a turn-on?

"The party-line has always been a car accident. Which is true, but I want to tell you the long version, so we don't have to revisit it," I finally answer him, looking up to gauge his expression. He nods before giving me a firm kiss on my lips.

"I want to know." His voice has dropped low, and he reaches over to tuck the blanket around my shoulders; not that it's necessary on a night like tonight.

"Mom liked her 'lunches with the ladies', she had them several days a week," I tell him, surprised at how dispassionate my tone sounds. There were so many days, I'd come home to find Mom passed out on the couch. "One day, she went from one of those, in the middle of a snowstorm, to pick Dad up from the airport and the car flipped on the way home.

"I was ten and thought nothing of the house being empty when I got home some days. It was after dinnertime, and I hadn't heard from either of them, so I put a frozen pizza in the oven because I was so hungry. I remember how aggravated I was that night, like, thinking that neither of my parents considered feeding me or were checking in to make sure I was even home? That's about when the cops rang the doorbell." I'm proud that I get that much out with my voice shaking, but I take a deep breath so I don't push my luck. "Mom hated her family, like absolutely despised them, so I had zero memory of them. Dad, well, it's just hard to explain, because you've met my grandparents now."

"Some people aren't meant to be parents, I think. It's not because they don't care, they're just wired differently," he offers. I can hear it in his voice that he doesn't want to overstep any boundary, yet he awkwardly tries to find words for the odd relationship I have with my grandparents.

"I only remember meeting them once before I was sent to live with them. It's not that Dad had bad memories, he was just apathetic to them. And to say that they were hands off when I was growing up is the understatement of the century. Again, it's not that they don't love me, they just never treated me like I was a child. If I needed something, I had to tell them. If I couldn't figure out how to do something, I would have to ask or figure it out on my own."

"Where did you grow up?" he asks me next. "You mentioned a snowstorm?"

"Minnesota," I reply succinctly. "And I was so excited to move here, until I tried to make friends with girls whose families have known each other for generations. It was hard at first, but I got there."

"Like your *close friend*, Di?" he chuckles.

"Ugh, no, I was happy she and her friends ignored me. At first, at least. By the time graduation rolled around, they all got very lovey, dovey. Almost sentimental in a way. Anyway, it's fine. It's nice that Di's Dad can bankroll my life for a while." I can't help the smirk that crosses my face, but I press my face into his neck in a lame attempt at hiding my snarky side.

"How about you? Were you part of the typical tight-knit group of kids that grew up together?" I ask him.

I can feel his pulse accelerate and immediately hope that I'm not crossing a line, finding myself on the other end of a deep question.

For the next quarter hour, he tells me about his best friend, Chains. Then even more about Chains' son, Josh. It sounds like being that baby's godfather means the world to him, and I tilt my head, studying his face as I try to picture him holding a baby.

"So, you want kids?" I ask him, wondering how his upbringing, life in a motorcycle club, and seeing his friend transition to a happy, family man has shaped his outlook.

"I don't know. I do know that if I have a choice in the matter, I'd want to bring the baby into a stable home. I know what my life was like, and I see how Nathan struggles with his daughter's mom. Maybe it's enough that I can be a solid uncle to whatever kids Nathan and Chains have."

"Alex and Josh are lucky to have you." I try to smile at him, but I'm not able to meet his eyes.

My heart started beating a weird tattoo the moment he started talking about his godson, and I have first-hand experience of the relationship he has with his niece. Even before my parents died, I've wanted a zillion kids. Hearing about his experience in a group home, opens my mind to taking in children, besides any biological children I may – someday – be blessed with.

When he kisses me on my forehead, I decide to table our discussion. The conversation has taken on a life of its own and after he made a point of telling me that, he's more or less, a rolling stone, talking about children on a first date seems more than a little crazy.

That was the first time he stayed the night with me, but hardly the last. Sometimes, Silver would be away for days, heading to Virginia to spend time with the Northern Grizzlies there. But he was a frequent guest at his brother's house and worked me into his life more and more.

"What are you doing next weekend?" he asks me the moment I pick up his call.

"I don't know, what am I doing next weekend?" I turn his question back on him.

"Funny you should ask. There's a whole weekend thing with my brothers up here and I want you to come with me," he replies, making me a little giddy that he wants to introduce me to some of the men I've heard so much about.

"Just out of curiosity, do I have any plans in the next few days?" I quiz him, keeping my voice light but hoping I don't have to wait a week to see him.

"If you're feeling frisky, I can be there tomorrow

afternoon." His voice deepens and I close my eyes, nearly moaning as I picture the wolfish grin he so often gives me.

"Silver? I'm definitely feeling frisky," I immediately reply.

"I'll text you before I leave, I want you ready for me–in that red number you have." Through the line, the demand and need in his tone makes my nipples hard enough to cut glass and I slide my hand down between my legs, hoping he has a little more time to talk.

"You tore the strap last week," I remind him.

"I'll pay you back if you replace it. Otherwise, naked works just as well." The roar of bikes near him nearly drowns out the end of his sentence, and I let out a sigh, knowing what's coming. "I gotta go, babe."

The next day doesn't grant me any time to go shopping, between helping my grandparents pack their truck for their road trip and then Di suddenly paid me for a project she had commissioned that I needed to double check before sending to her. That left me with just enough time to shower and prepare for his arrival.

I may be doing this out of order, because we hadn't talked about whether he was sleeping with anyone else, but I was ready to have sex with him and more than trusted him to know what he was doing in that department.

Since I'm not nearly brave enough to meet him at

the door naked, I text him that my door will be unlocked, and he should be clever enough to find me.

Not long after that, I hear his bike pulling up outside and my breath catches as I strain to hear him climbing the stairs.

"Marco…" he calls out and I smile when I hear him bolt the door.

"Polo…" Okay, I'm apparently a huge coward, I think as I change my mind and yank the covers up over my body.

Then I tilt my head, wondering why he's not in my room yet; at least until I hear two thuds and then the sound of his belt buckle jangling. Well, if he's stripping out there, I can at least show a little skin, I decide. Rolling onto my side, I throw a leg over the cover while keeping most of my front covered.

I'm about to call 'Marco' when I hear him in the bathroom, and I grin in anticipation.

At long last, he's standing in my bedroom doorway and takes a moment to trace my body with his eyes. The dark boxers contrast beautifully with his skin, at least the areas without tattoos, and I bite my lower lip, excited by his abs and muscular chest.

"You're so fucking beautiful," he growls, closing the tiny distance between us and squatting between my bed and the wall as he runs his hand through my hair.

"I want you, Sam," I tell him, letting the blanket fall away as I reach for him. I know he prefers Silver, but here with me, in bed, I decide he's going to be Sam and not the nickname the world uses for him.

"Yeah?" he confirms, leaning in for a soft kiss and I'm nodding even as our lips touch.

When he shifts, moving toward my pussy, I stop him; my hand on his chin as I shake my head.

"Not that today," I murmur, reaching down for his cock. "Just this."

He raises an eyebrow at me before reaching his hand down to my pussy. The moment he feels how wet I am, he covers me with his body and before I know it, he's nudging his hard, wrapped cock against my folds.

Gently at first, he slides up and down, until the emptiness inside me is driving me out of my mind. I bend my knees, and angle myself, as though begging him to enter me without saying a word. Finally, his mouth covers mine, more demanding than normal as he shifts his hips back before he thrusts completely into me.

There's a slight pinch with his intrusion and I wrap my limbs around him, never wanting to feel empty again.

"You okay?" he whispers against my lips.

"Yes," I answer, kissing every bit of his flesh that I can reach, until he tilts my chin up so we're eye to eye.

"I almost feel bad for you," his jaw clenches tight as he spits out each word and my heart goes into overdrive, wondering what I did wrong. "As long as I'm alive, I'm the only man who's ever going to fuck this pussy."

His words light a fire in me and although impossible, I try to pull him deeper inside of me as I clench the walls of my tunnel around his dick. I lean up to bite his lip, and he doesn't pause when our teeth hit; he just holds me tightly against him, before he proceeds to pound into me like he's pissed off.

"I can't stay the night, but you're going to feel me for days, aren't you, Maggie?" He grinds out the words.

"Harder, Sam," I moan, and almost feel like I'm baiting him as he pants above me. I kick a foot down on his ass and he leans in to suck on my neck. Holy shit! No gentle lovemaking for my first time. "I can take it!"

I let out a shriek when he pulls completely out of me, grabbing my shoulder to roll me over and he nudges in between my thighs, spanking my ass when I don't move fast enough. Exhaling when I feel him deeper than he was a moment ago, I grin into the pillow as he picks up the speed again.

It's the feel of him pinching my nipples that have me pushing up from the bed, feeling as though there's a current running between the sensitive tips down to my clit. I thrust back, eagerly meeting him until I throw my head back, screaming out my release.

He chuckles behind me, gradually slowing down

until he collapses on top of me. At least once, it seems like he tries to shift his weight off of me, but I refuse to let him, even as heavy as he is, it feels too good.

"Sam?"

He grunts in reply. Moving his hips back, I can hear him removing the condom before pulling a sheet between his cock and my ass.

"I don't want you with anyone else, while we're doing this." While I had previously played with different ways to ask him not to cheat on me, the words come out as a demand and strike me how territorial I feel after what just happened between us.

"That's only fair, because I goddamn meant what I said, Maggie," his words are whispered in my ear and are anything but the sweet promises sometimes given in these situations. "We're not a casual thing, not anymore."

I wiggle around to face him, the sheet twisting around somehow keeps our bodies cool as it soaks up our sweat. The determination and hard lines on his face seem so different than Silver's typical, happy-go-lucky expression and I realize that by inviting Sam to my bed, that's who I got. My smile eases the storm in his eyes, and my kiss reverts back to the gentle, teasing ones we usually share.

"I'm good with that," I whisper when we come up for air.

Sam and I have enough in common that I understand what it's like to have your world turned upside down. We both know that a lifetime of tomorrows isn't guaranteed and the best we can do, is to promise to be with the other, as long as we can. And now *I* know, that when the day comes that one of us must go on without the other, it won't happen because the other stopped holding on, it will mean the other was ripped away.

Eventually, he gets up and goes back to the bathroom before returning to clean me up with a wet cloth and breaking the news that he's due in Georgia tonight.

With a promise of a longer visit when he returns, Sam tucks me in and I quickly fall asleep.

SILVER

My phone pings and I look down at it to see a text from Maggie letting me know she's heading up the drive. I had told Nathan days beforehand that I had wanted him to meet her and in typical Nathan fashion, he said nothing, and just went about his business.

Yesterday morning, he casually mentioned that Alex wanted his pulled pork for dinner on her next overnight and I might as well invite *my woman* over also. That was all good and well, until earlier when I went down to unlock the gate for her, and he acted like I was trying to topple the government.

"Nate, I told her to get here between four and five,

I'm not going to sit down there and wait for her. Just fucking relax." I sigh in frustration, rubbing my hand through my hair.

Alex lets out a little laugh and we both turn our frowns on her. "You two are like mirror images sometimes," she says, holding her hands up in surrender. "Silver, haven't you figured out by now that Dad didn't come with the 'relax' setting?"

"Maybe we could try the factory reset option?" I innocently ask her, and she taps her lips with a finger as she considers that possibility.

"Okay, you distract him, then I'll jump him," she loudly whispers across the room to me. "Where do you think his button is?"

"You're grounded," Nathan growls, but we both see the glint in his eye as he stalks back to the kitchen.

I share a smile with Alex, knowing he's all bark and no bite when it comes to her.

"I think he was talking to you," she deadpans, and there's no mistaking the chuckle this pulls from her father.

"And I have a feeling you've already hit all of his buttons," I tease her back, reaching out to tousle her hair.

And now, with Maggie on her way up the driveway, I find myself unaccountably nervous. I want this to go well, just like I want this Christmas to go off without a hitch. Chains, Sophia, and Josh will be flying out here to meet Nathan and Alex – and Maggie, too, if she hasn't dumped my ass by then.

"She's here!" Alex needlessly calls out.

I cross the room to get out to her Jeep first, but am momentarily blocked by Nathan as he carries a tray of sides out to the grill. He takes one look at her, then bellows over his shoulder.

"Alex! Your playdate is here!"

Maggie's eyes widen and twin spots of red bloom on her cheeks, I groan, suddenly understanding how she felt when her grandmother put on a show to embarrass her the first time we hung out.

"Nathan, this is Maggie, she's here to interview you about saving…" I have Maggie smiling ear to ear as I give my brother shit, but it's when he slams the food down and cusses a blue streak that I decide to lay off. "Kidding. Maggie why don't you come in and officially meet Alex, while my brother gets his temper under control?"

"Is she armed today?" Maggie asks, giving Nathan a little wave as she climbs the porch steps, and I'm surprised to see a large purse hanging from her shoulder since she usually doesn't carry one. I shrug it off as a girl thing when she stretches up on her tiptoes to give me a quick kiss on the cheek.

"No, all clear," I promise her, turning to lead her inside.

"Perfect," she murmurs and I'm trying to piece that

comment together when I hear Nathan howl with laughter from the doorway, just before Alex lets out a scream.

Maggie must have gotten two or three Nerf rounds off before I understood she was using my body as cover when she pulled the toy gun out of her purse and took aim at my niece. Maggie keeps firing until Alex is able to throw herself behind a couch, then when I turn to look at her, she hits me smack in the middle of my forehead with a lucky shot. Lucky, because she didn't take my eye out.

"Hey!" I grab the gun from her and start to turn it on her before realizing it's empty. That's when the first blast of silly string hits my face. Maggie used my distraction to her advantage, dammit. I don't want to think about having to clean it off my Northern Grizzlies cut. "Not my…"

"Not in the house." Nathan makes use of the tone he typically reserves for his daughter, as he deftly grabs the can out of her hand and mumbles about children today not having any manners. He crosses to place the silly string out of reach as I place the gun on the coffee table.

"Is it safe to come out?" Alex calls out from where she retreated.

"Nicely played, babe," I say, stalking toward Maggie, and she reads my intent clear as day, trying to keep me at arm's length. Fortunately, Nathan had the foresight to close the door, so she doesn't have anywhere to go.

By the time I've finished kissing her, the green string is smeared across both of our faces and all I can think of is how to cut this dinner short and get back to her place.

"If you two are done, go get cleaned up. Alex, quit your gawking and go turn the corn and stir the beans," Nathan's voice sounds stern, but his daughter and I know better.

I grab Maggie's hand to bring her to the cabin's sole bathroom.

"Is Nathan pissed at me?" she asks in a hushed tone.

"Impressed, more like it," I assure her, standing behind her as I turn on the water and she reaches for the soap.

Teasing aside, we help each other clean our hands and faces, sharing kisses in between. It's only my brother's sudden banging on the door that gets us moving.

The meal goes well, with Nathan slowly relaxing as Alex heats up the brownies she made and goes to select a board game for us. It's when he silently excuses himself, that I realize he stepped away to tend to his nightly ritual of making sure the gate was secure.

I'm not sure that he sees me looking out of the window, but when I see him go to start the fire in the smaller cabin that he and I have been fixing up, I understand that he's fine with Maggie staying on his land overnight, and wants her to be comfortable.

It's the closest thing to a seal of approval that he'll ever give anyone. And his way of telling me that he likes us together.

FIVE

MAGGIE

CHRISTMAS 2023

"What's bothering you, Maggie May?" my grandpa asks, and I jump in surprise, looking down at the eggs that I had cracked into a bowl but hadn't started whisking.

I just shake my head, not really sure how to express myself or how much he wants to hear.

Yesterday, Silver's best friend and his family arrived and spent the night settling into Nathan's cabin and getting to know him and his daughter. Last week, when my grandmother had heard the plans, she had insisted that everyone come here tomorrow, for Christmas. It made sense, and considering the size of this house, they all even agreed to stay the night.

Ever since Silver had put me in touch with Sophia, I've enjoyed our conversations that have slowly turned into FaceTiming every few days. Thankfully, she liked my work enough to put me in touch with other authors and I've been able to break into an area I had never considered – the indie book world.

When I met Nathan, I was more intimidated by him than nervous. He's even bigger than Silver, and rougher around the edges. It's meeting Chains that has set my nerves on edge.

While Nathan might be Silver's blood, I've heard enough about Chains to know that he's truly Silver's brother. I've never been so worried about someone liking me before.

Silver has texted me several times today, asking me to head up to Nathan's, but I keep rotating between three excuses to give myself more time. Well, I had to cut that down to two, he called me laughing after I said I was helping Grandma with the meal prep.

Completely valid reaction.

Grandpa startles me when he gently removes the whisk from my hands and slides the bowl over to take up the task I started.

"I couldn't stand that turd you dated a bit in high school," he starts talking, low and calm as usual. "Your granny told me to keep my nose out of it, though."

"He was the best of the lot," I answer with a harsh chuckle. "They just all seemed so childish to me."

"Silver is a man through and through, one that seems to know his mind," Grandpa says, pointing toward the other ingredients I had laid out and I start to carefully measure each item. "He's respectful to you, and us. You said you had a good time when he brought you to Virginia for that party at the Northern Grizzlies' place, right?"

"Yeah, they were like this big crazy family. It was a little overwhelming at first, but I never felt left out," I respond, smiling at the memory of the ride up there and the antics of the men I came to know over the course of the weekend and a couple of times since then.

Silver had introduced me around and even when he'd go talk to some of the others, he'd come and check on me every so often. At least until the local president's sister, Bridget, had shooed him away, taking me under her wing. I was more than a little surprised when she reached out to me afterwards, putting me to work on creating graphics for Northern Grizzlies gear. The online store she envisioned for the seven chapters will roll out early next year, and I'll get a nice cut of the profits.

"What makes you think this other friend of his is going to take one look at you and do something to screw up your relationship?" he asks, and I smile at his way of invoking other memories before smacking me with the issue at hand.

"Because, his opinion holds the most weight," I whisper my fear so softly that I'm not even sure my grandpa can hear me.

Just then there's a brief knock on the kitchen door before it swings open and a man is backing into our kitchen, his familiar cut identifies him seconds before I see Silver's face over his shoulder.

"Silver called about bringing the ham over today," my grandfather suddenly thinks to tell me. "Just to make things easier when they all come tomorrow."

I simply stand there as they maneuver the cooler into the kitchen and set it on the floor, it's the smile that Silver gives me that makes me realize that I hadn't stopped pouring the flour into the measuring cup when my head had turned toward the door.

"Your cup runneth over there, babe," he cracks, nodding toward the flour I've spilled everywhere.

"Crap!" I put both items down and clap my hands together, trying to clean them off a little. "Dammit, I..."

Looking between the mess and the men, I can't help but notice the stranger, who has to be Chains, coming straight to me, his arms extended for a hug.

"Come here," he says, grinning ear to ear, even when I hold up my messy hands to stop his approach. "I don't give a shit, you're like my sister now!"

His laughter is infectious, as his warmth and in

seconds, he's spinning me in a circle. "Damn, Maggie, now I understand why he barely comes home anymore. Sophia can't wait to meet you either. In person, that is, she always talks about you like you've been friends for years."

"That's enough now," Silver grumbles, pulling me into his arms. It's right before he kisses me that I see the look on my grandpa's face and my heart swells. His little chat had two purposes, one to let me know I was with the right person, the other, so I wouldn't freak out waiting for the guys to show up.

"Well, *Merry Christmas*!" my grandma practically purrs, checking out Chains as she joins us. "I must have been a very good girl to get three handsome men in my kitchen."

"Just wait, Nathan'll be here tomorrow," Silver teases her, drawing in his breath when I elbow him.

"Don't encourage her, you nimwit," Grandpa grumbles from beside us.

"Mrs. Dennison, it's very nice to meet you. I'm Cal Fromm." Chains steps forward to introduce himself and it's the first time I've heard his given name.

I have to smile when he flips on his manners, knowing that his uncle drummed them into Silver and Chains when they were boys. Silver squeezes me to get my attention, tilting his head toward the door when I look up at him.

We slide out, leaving Chains behind chatting with my grandparents.

"Come here," he says, tugging me over to the truck they came here in. "You alright?"

"Yeah, I'm good. I think I just freaked myself out," I admit. He opens the door and pulls me to lean against him, shielding us from the wind that has kicked up today.

"I thought you were getting cold feet about us, but Sophia assured me that you're head over heels for me," Silver says. The smile on his face is only marred by the worry I see in his eyes. He pulls a rectangular black box from the bin on the inside of the car door. "Then I thought, I should give you this today instead of tomorrow."

"Silver!" Not that I didn't think he'd get me a present, but I didn't think we were at the jewelry stage already.

"Open it," he says, sounding excited.

It's a silver necklace with the infinity symbol and I smile up at him as I hurry to put it on. "Thank you."

"I wanted something to remind you that I love you and I want us to be together. I hope this isn't too much, too soon, but it's how I feel." He smiles as he centers the pendant between my collar bones at my throat.

"I've wanted to tell you that I loved you since the first time you went to Bingo with us," I confess in a rush, leaning up to kiss him so he won't see the tears in my eyes.

"Sorry to interrupt," Chains says from behind us. "Soph texted me a couple of things she needs from the store before it closes and Diane gave me a list of things that you're in charge of, Maggie."

Although they drop me off less than an hour later, I'm already completely comfortable with Chains and looking forward to the next day. This time it's harder to turn down Silver's offer of spending the night up at Nathan's place, but I'm not going to bail on my grand-parents with so many chores left before the feast tomorrow.

"I can take him upstairs," Chains offers, approaching the couch where his son and I are sitting.

Not long after dinner and presents, Josh had announced that I *needed* to tell him a story and had dragged me over to a quiet corner. For lack of any idea of what story was appropriate, I started creating one and after his very detailed questions about the made-up people stopped, I realized that he had conked out.

The weight of his small body was comforting, so I didn't bother to try to signal anyone for help, knowing one of his parents would come looking eventually. "Only if you don't wake him," I whisper back.

"Nah, once he's out he won't move until daylight," Chains replies, squatting beside us instead of trying to pick up his son. "I'm glad he met you when he did, Maggie."

Tilting my head, I think about what his words mean before nodding. "Silver wouldn't have stopped long enough, if he hadn't found his brother," I say softly. "That's how he was before, wasn't he?"

"Sophia thinks everything happens at a set time. Like the universe waits for all these random pieces to align, then we find that perfect job, or car, or person," he says, his face showing his doubt about this theory. "Who knows. But, then that vlogger's stupid video, um, great production on your end, reunites him with Nathan and brings you into his orbit. If I look at it that way, I won't be able to tease Soph next time she tries to make her point."

"I forgot y'all saw that." I laugh, more at his attempt to save my feelings over Di's vlog. "Unfortunately, Di is in St. Barts this Christmas with her parents, so you won't get to meet her. She's been after me to bring her to the Northern Grizzlies clubhouse, she wants to do a segment on *biker gangs*."

Josh shifts in his sleep, his elbow jamming into my bladder. "Oh, I'm going to need you to move him now!" I say urgently yet softly.

Showing that he's done this many times, Chains quickly has his son in one arm and reaches a hand down to help me up. "Well, what I wanted to say, is welcome to the family. I'm really happy he's found his other half."

With that, he turns and heads upstairs. When I aim toward my grandparents' bathroom, I see Silver watching us and blow him a kiss. He steps in my direction, which turns into a near chase as I really do need the bathroom.

He thumps the door that's closed in his face, but I can hear him through the wood panel as I sit down to pee. "Did he say anything too embarrassing?"

"He just wanted to tell me about how you keep a woman at each of the chapters. As long as I'm happy getting you for seven and a half weeks a year, we should work out great," I tell him and hear his grunt.

"Well, you were bound to find out sooner or later," he deadpans. "Oh, and the kids."

"That's where I'm having a problem," I pipe up, trying to keep the laughter from my voice. "I mean ten or fifteen, you know that's something I could get used to, but thirty-one?"

"You have until the count of five and I'm coming in," he announces, and I hurry to clean up since there's no lock on the door.

"Hey! That was four," I whine as I turn on the faucet.

"Ah, I was hoping to catch you with your pants down." The cocky grin he gives me is his mask, his eyes dark as they watch me—in this case, making sure that I was just giving him shit and not worried or jealous over anything I may have heard from Chains.

"Just so we're clear, you're just getting me and considering my age, I come with little-to-no baggage." His words vibrate along my neck as he kisses his way up to my earlobe.

"Yeah, more like a shaving kit than baggage, really," I tease him. The man must be pictured in the dictionary under 'traveling light'.

"But, if we do get a house, and I'm being honest, I'd really like to start with getting a dog. Would you be good with that? For starters?" He sounds so damn hopeful that it stirs up the butterflies in my tummy.

"Oh, I've always wanted a puppy!" I coo, turning into his arms and wiping my hands on his flannel shirt. "I think, that if you don't leave me along the side of the road this summer, I'd love to get a dog with you."

"You'll be the best dog momma," he whispers and tries to kiss me, but my laugh makes that impossible.

"I think you just called me a bitch."

"For the record, I meant that you were *my bitch,* even though I was hoping you wouldn't notice." The feel of his hands cupping my breasts have me lifting my leg up to circle his hip.

There's a sudden rapping on the door before

Nathan calls out, "What's with you two and bath-rooms? Come on, I gotta use it."

My cheeks are bright red when we exit and while I was hoping to sneak by Nathan, he puts a hand on each of my shoulders to give me a squeeze. "He's a lucky man, Maggie. If he ever needs reminding, I'll be the first in line to knock some sense into him."

"Thank you, Nathan," I shyly answer, leaning up to kiss his rough cheek. "I'm going to hold you to that."

After that, my grandparents say their goodnights and Chains 'hires' Alex to babysit his sleeping son, then the five of us take all the remaining beer and wine to my small apartment.

Silver and Chains keep the rest of us entertained, reliving their childhood adventures over the hours that flow into dawn—we subtly exchange smiles and winks, enjoying the connection they have.

One that has shifted from two, nearly orphaned boys, to bind Nathan, Sophia, and me into their brotherhood.

PART TWO

SPRING OF 2024

SIX

SILVER

"You've been spending a lot of time with that girl," Vector says, no doubt about to introduce the subject that's come up more and more this spring. Subtlety is not one of his strong points and I know that both he and Jasper have given me plenty of leeway as far as spending time first with my brother, and now with Maggie, since she's become a fixture in my life.

My phone rings with a number I don't recognize, and I look around the table at Vector, Oak, and Roman, then down at the cards in my hand. Staring at them any longer won't change how much they suck, so I throw my hand down and finally click the accept button because it's the same area code as Yanceyville.

"Hello, I'm trying to reach a Samuel Rawlings," a

woman's voice comes over the line and while my initial instinct is to hang up, her voice is strained and all I can think is how tired and upset she sounds.

"This is he," I answer, standing up and walking outside so I can hear better.

"Mr. Rawlings, I'm Anita Mayor with Caswell County's social services," she pauses, as though trying to find the right words and that's when I hear the soft sobbing in the background. "I have Alexandria Rawlings here and need to find a family member who will assume care of her, or I'll have to find her space in a group home."

"What the hell's going on? Where's Nathan?" The words burst out of my mouth as I feel my heart contracting and the world tilting on its axis.

As the silence drags on, somehow, I just know the answer.

"Let me talk to him," Alex calls out. Her voice is barely recognizable as she continues to cry in the background.

"Mr. Rawlings, the local police were supposed to contact you. I'm very sorry to be the one to tell you that your brother is dead."

My brother. For the first time since my initial weeks in foster care, I feel my eyes welling up with tears.

I just got him back. We haven't had enough time. Is this really happening?

"Silver? Silver, are you there?" The pain in Alex's

voice finally cuts through the fog in my head and I look up to see Vector in front of me, his hand reaching down for my phone—making me wonder how long I've been standing here.

That's when I realize I'm not even standing, I'm crouched down, leaning against the building.

"I'm here, Alex," I respond, gradually coming back to the here and now. "I'm so sorry, sweet girl."

"It was awful," she sobs out. "And they want to make me go stay with strangers, but we found your number."

My head snaps up. No fucking way is Alex going to experience what I did as a child!

"I'm a couple of hours away, but I'll get there before nightfall and we'll stay at your dad's house..." My words are cut off by more loud crying on her side and I wonder where the fuck her mother is this time.

"That's where she killed him!" I can barely make out Alex's words, then I hear a man's voice in the background.

"Mr. Rawlings? I'm the retired sheriff, name's Carter, the current sheriff was on his way to Maggie Dennison's house to try to notify you, but I just got word he was in an accident on the drive over. It appears that your brother's ex and her friend attacked and killed Nathan. We have her in custody. Unfortunately, her friend remains at large." By the time Carter has finished talking, I feel steadier, so I push myself back up and nod at Vector before I place the call on the speaker setting.

"I'm going to call Maggie now, then get on the road. It'll take me about two hours to get there. Does my niece have any other next of kin that I need to worry about?" I ask him, my eyes locked on Vector even as Roman approaches us.

"Her maternal grandmother has already told social serv…" his voice cuts off for a moment and is noticeably softer when he starts talking again. "Sorry, shit. I'm going to level with you, I retired a few months back and the deputies in town are straight out of the academy. Shit went sideways the moment a deer hit Sheriff Tusco's car. Alright, I'm far enough away from your niece."

With that he draws a long breath in before continuing. "The town council called me when they got word that Tusco was en route to the hospital and no one else knew how to work a crime scene. The only good news is that I have worked in this area enough to know Nathan and his ex, Prim. She was running with all the wrong people after they ended things and honestly, I always thought it would be her that'd wind up dead. Anyway, Prim's mother told social services she won't take Alexandria. I understand you're dating Maggie Dennison. I've known her grandparents for years and out of respect for what's happening, if they agree, I'll drop Alexandria off there and post a deputy outside until you arrive."

"I would appreciate that," I tell him, pleased that he's willing to bend a few rules for me. Cop or not, I'm going to try to keep on his good side no matter how longwinded he is. "Can I speak to Alex again for a minute?"

Expecting another monologue, I take it as a win that Alex's voice is the next one I hear.

"Silver?"

"I'm going to leave now and call Maggie the second I hit the road, Carter said he'd get you to her house," I tell her, closing my eyes and wishing I had some idea about how to comfort her.

"What's going to happen to me?"

Gone is the vivacious girl that held me at gunpoint the first time we met and my heart breaks with her words.

"We're family, Alex. You're going to have to go easy on me, but if you'll have me, we'll figure out how I can adopt you." With those words, she makes a noise that sounds like a cross between a laugh and a sob.

"Be careful getting here," Alex whispers and I grunt before disconnecting the call.

"You need some company?" Vector asks me from where he took a seat on the steps. I barely consider it before I shake my head.

"Naw, it's too close to the Knight's territory. Losing one brother today sucks bad enough," I answer him. "Could you let Jasper know though? My brother's ex and some bum she runs with murdered him. I gotta call Maggie and let her know that Alex is going to be dropped off with her and I just don't have the bandwidth to keep explaining this until I have all the details."

"Silver," Vector calls out before I slide onto my bike. "Being a single parent has its challenges, but its rewards also."

I nod before pulling my helmet on and pairing my Bluetooth. Maggie and I have been enjoying each other's company for months now, and as much as Nathan liked to give me shit that she's closer in age to Alex than she is to me, this next call is going to make or break us.

MAGGIE

"I was just thinking about you." I have long since worried about sounding over-eager when Silver calls. He seems to pause whatever he was going to say and as the silence drags on, I can hear the thrum of the road in the background. "Where are you heading now?"

"Maggie," the way he utters my name like he's gasping for breath sends my heart rate into overdrive and I stand up, looking out of my window like danger is approaching. "Honey, I don't know when they'll be there, but can you take Alex in when the cops drop her off?"

"Cops? I will, of course, but what's happening?" I wonder if I'll be able to hear his response over the intense beating noise my heart is making. "Is she alright?"

"Everything is fucked," he replies. "Nathan was murdered, his ex was arrested, and I just got on the road."

"Silver, I need you to listen to me," I say, trying to keep my voice even, as adrenaline shoots through my veins. The thought of him on the road after getting that news terrifies me. "You need to get here safely. Take deep breaths and focus on your surroundings. Everything is fucked, absolutely. I'm here if talking will keep you calm, but it might be best if I go and prepare my grandparents for her arrival."

"I'll be fine," he tells me, even though it sounds like he's strangling on the words.

"I'll call you when Alex is here."

"Thank you," he whispers before the line goes dead.

Holy shit! How could this have happened? I picture Nathan making s'mores with his daughter just a couple of weeks ago, as we all enjoyed a beautiful evening.

Pulling on a hoodie, more for comfort than warmth, I wiggle into my slippers and quickly cross the driveway to the main house.

"Good Lord, Maggie!" Gran yells as I accidentally throw open the kitchen door harder than I mean to. The noise had her turning away from the open refrigerator door and grabbing her lower back. "What is going on?"

"Where's Grandpa? It'll be easier to explain this…"

"I'm right here," Grandpa's loud voice comes from directly behind me and now it's my turn to scream in surprise. I swear it's like the thought of him just conjures the man sometimes.

"I'm buying you bells for your birthday," I mumble, ignoring Gran's raised eyebrow and the how-do-you-like-it? look that she's shooting me.

"Did you need us?" Grandpa asks, prompting me back to the matter at hand.

"Alex, Silver's niece, is going to be dropped off here in a little bit and one of the deputies will be keeping watch outside," I start with the most relevant information.

"Which deputy?" Gran asks me before I can continue.

"I don't know, that isn't the point…"

"Of course, it is, I have to start cooking and that Lenny character has a peanut allergy," Gran replies, cutting me off again and waving her hands in frustration, either at Lenny's peanut allergy or my lack of details, I'm not sure. "This isn't very much notice."

"Diane?" Grandpa gently calls her name, all the

while watching my face. "I think we need to listen to what Maggie has to say before you start your cooking."

With a subtle nod in his direction, I turn my focus on my grandma. "Silver's brother was murdered today, by Alex's mother. Alex doesn't have anyone else, so Silver needs us to watch her until he can get here and figure things out. They may need to stay for a little while, I really don't have any other details right now."

"Oh!" Gran crosses to hug me, as though I'm the one who needs comfort, while Grandpa makes a face over her shoulder.

"Thankfully, Alex isn't allergic to peanuts," he cracks, and I close my eyes, hoping they get this nonsense out of their system before she gets here.

"Not the time, Fred!" Gram snaps at him, turning away from him and reaching for her peanut oil. "But yes, you said she liked that chicken I sent over there, didn't you? I have chicken already defrosted and Lenny will just have to take his chances."

"It could be Melinda they're sending with her," Grandpa helpfully adds. I pinch the bridge of my nose, wondering at what age I might start to exhibit their special brand of crazy. "I'll go make sure the guest rooms aren't too dusty and get them towels. Will Silver want my shotgun, or will he come armed?"

"Do you think we'll be under siege?" Gran asks me, but one look at her tells me she's not expecting an answer. "If I had known we'd have guests, I would have gone to the supermarket today."

"I love you, Grandma," I say, letting out a loud sigh as I seek to remind myself of that fact. "Thank you for opening your home."

"You have to act like everything is normal, you know." I'm only half listening to her, but her next words send chills down my back. "Let her have a good cry, then get her into a routine. She's a little older than you were when you lost your parents, but normalcy is just as important at her age."

And thinking back, that's exactly what she and Grandpa had done when I was dropped on their doorstep. They let me cry one day, then asked me to help them with the laundry the next. From that second day, our routine was: school, homework, chores, a fun activity for the three of us on Saturday, and church on Sunday. As I made friends in this town and found hobbies I wanted to explore, my routine expanded, but the core stayed the same.

"Even if things don't work out with you and Silver, you should consider remaining a part of her life, maybe if only a text now and then. She's always going to remember today, so a piece of you will stay with her, keep that in mind, my love," Gran continues as she starts to gather ingredients for one of her cakes.

Even if she's a little nutty, Gran is definitely insightful, and her unsolicited advice sounds pretty damn good to me. From behind, I wrap my arms around her shoulders and kiss her cheek. "Thank you."

"It looks like they sent Melinda along with old Carter," Grandpa calls out. "Good to know you won't be responsible for killing that poor Lenny today. Maggie, why don't you come greet them and I'll bring some beverages into the living room. Tomorrow, we can bring Alex to the grocery store to pick out what she likes."

"The next town over, fewer people will recognize her that way," Gran murmurs, nodding her head.

I pull open the front door to see Alex looking out the passenger seat window of an older truck. Crossing the walk, I hold a hand out in her direction and she attempts to pull the edges of her mouth up into a grin, but ends up crying harder as she opens the door and leaps out, running into my arms.

"Come on inside, sweetheart," I whisper into her ear, nodding at our retired sheriff over her shoulder. As I guide her toward the formal living room, Grandpa steps outside to join Carter on the porch.

Smiling, I see that Grandpa had brought out a couple of cans from his *secret* stash of root beer. My mind scrambles as I try to figure out what to say, and just as I'm about to open my mouth to fill the silence between us, I realize that this is all she needs right now. Silence, and someone she knows holding her as she cries.

Nothing I can say or do will change a damn thing, so I just stay beside her, stroking her back as her tears soak through the fabric of my hoodie. We both jump when the phone in my front pocket rings and I reach into the pouch to pull it out.

"It's your uncle, honey," I say as I answer the call. "Hey, she just got here a few minutes ago."

"Does she need anything?" No sooner does he ask that, than he clicks his tongue. "Fuck, yeah, she needs her dad."

"It's a new road for everyone, Silver. Just take it slow as you learn the twists and turns," I reply, ever so slightly channeling my grandma.

"Good advice, Yoda," he says, chuckling. "Put me on speaker?"

"Here she is," I tell him, once I've adjusted the setting and I decide to let her know what our tentative plan is. "Alex, are you alright staying here with us the next few days? You can have the same room you stayed in at Christmas, if you like?"

"Just until I figure out what to do," Silver's voice comes through the speaker, along with the noise from the road.

"That might take more than a few days," Alex responds with a hiccup at the end.

I try to hide my smile at the sudden resurfacing of her sass.

"True, but let's keep in mind that Mrs. Dennison is a much better cook than I am, so it's a win-win, as long as we don't overstay our welcome." As wary as he sounds, I can make out the bare hint of relief in his voice. Their banter seems to bring them both comfort, I think, as she lets out a heavy sigh.

"Speaking of which, Grandma is making her famous chicken, *and* a cake," I pick up the conversation when she doesn't reply and that's when I notice the specks of blood on her clothing. My eyes move to her hands and my heart skips a beat when I see more of the dried blood on them. "I'm going to get Alex into the shower before we eat, but, Silver, we promise to save you some."

"I'll be there as soon as I can," he promises.

"Safely," Alex says, leaning against me again.

"Safely," he repeats before disconnecting the call.

"He doesn't know how to be a dad." Alex's voice is so soft I barely hear it as I lead her up the creaky stairs.

"I don't think anyone knows how to be a parent, until they are," I tell her. "He is going to need a little bit of a learning curve, though."

"What about you?" she asks, barely sparing a glance at the room I lead her to.

"What about me?"

"If he's raising me, is, I mean, I don't know, are you two going to stay together?"

I knew that some form of that question was coming, but was hoping that Silver would be here so we could play hot potato with it. Lacking his presence, I reach my hand up to trace the infinity symbol on the necklace he gave me.

"That's a pretty big question, and one that he and I need to discuss before you and I talk about it. Come to think of it, there are going to be a lot of big questions over the next few weeks, some we'll have answers for and some we won't. At least, not right away. We'll all just do our best, okay?"

"If you two break up, can we still talk?"

"For the record, I love Silver, and you. And my answer is, absolutely," I promise her, and she throws her arms around me as she starts to cry again. "Come on, you get into the shower and I'm going to run to my apartment to find you some clean clothes."

With that she stills before loudly sniffling and drawing back from me.

"I didn't get to bring anything from home," she says hesitantly, keeping her eyes downcast. "It's a crime scene so I couldn't and…"

"I'm not giving you my black jeans," I tell her firmly, immediately guessing what her game is. Alex's eyes fly wide open, surprised by how quickly I caught on to what she was leading up to.

"It was worth a try." She shrugs her shoulders before picking up the towels that were left on the bed.

"Take your time, I'll leave the clothes on that chair and my grandparents and I will be in the keeping room," I tell her, pulling on one of her disheveled braids.

"Um, could you stay up here with me?" she asks, hesitating to leave the room. "I mean after you find some clothes? Then we can go down together."

"Of course, Alex," I tell her, kicking myself for not thinking of how she wouldn't want to be alone right now.

The headlight on Silver's bike illuminates the faintly lit living room, well after we've had our meal, and my grandparents have retired to their room. Alex has been in and out of sleep for the past hour or so, her lower legs on my lap as she rests her head on a few of the cross-stitch pillows my gran collects.

I watch him as he gets off of his bike and stretches, staring, unblinking, at the house until he finally spots me as I crane my head in his direction. He nods once before turning to check in with the cop assigned to watch over us.

Not sure what I should do, I decide to try to have a word with Silver before Alex wakes up again, so I slide around the edge and tip toe toward the door, meeting him on the porch.

He's already at the bottom step and within seconds, his arms are wrapped around me as he buries his face into the crook of my neck.

"Thank you," he says so softly, I can barely make out the words. "How is she?"

"How are you?" I ask in return.

"This fucking sucks." He laughs bitterly, tightening his arms around me.

"It does, there's not a thing I can say to make any of it better, sweetheart, but I'll be here to listen and help," I promise him. My heart is fit to bursting, wanting to reassure him of my feelings but knowing he has other priorities and needs right now. "She's on the couch, the two upstairs bedrooms are set up for you both, and there are leftovers in the fridge."

"What should I say?"

"I've been kinda winging it, but Grandma insists that getting her into a routine, including chores, is important. It wasn't until this afternoon that I realized how they dealt with the ten-year-old girl who was dropped on their doorstep," I tell him.

"Well, they didn't fuck you up, so it's worth a try,"

he counters, kissing my cheek before stepping back and bracing himself. Exhaling a deep breath, his hand wrapped around my neck, he nods to himself. "Will you wait for me in the kitchen? In case I need back up?"

"Absolutely," I nod, then open the door so he can go in to wake Alex.

I slide inside after him, quietly moving to the kitchen to wait for him. My heart aches, not only for what Alex is going to be facing but for Silver. After searching for his brother for so many years, Nathan's death has to be devasting to him now.

SEVEN

SILVER

"Fred," I say, acknowledging the man who's having coffee in the kitchen before the sun is up. Granted, it is his house, but coming upon him in his underwear is a little off-putting.

"Sam," he greets me, never having warmed up to my road name. He juts his chin out in the direction of my jeans, and I reach down, finding the zipper open.

Considering that I'm sneaking back inside after fucking his granddaughter half the night, I guess I need to reevaluate the man's right to wear his briefs wherever he wants to.

"I have a meeting with the sheriff today, he should have a date when Alex and I can move into Nathan's house." Today's the fourth day we've been here, and I had no idea it would take this long. I had run Alex to the apartment she and her mom stayed in, so she could get her things, but there was no way I was going to move into that dump.

"You let Diane know what he says. She and some of the ladies from church are all prepared to go in there and clean everything up," he tells me and the dumbfounded expression on my face has him raising an eyebrow at me. "The police don't clean up the crime scene, you know. And we're willing to bet they made a bigger mess of things during their investigation."

"I hadn't considered it," I state the obvious. "I can't thank you and Diane enough for all you've done, and now, thinking of this."

"It's all those crime shows she likes to watch. They're not just to keep me in line, I guess," he responds, chuckling a bit before he continues. "But like I tell my buddies, if it looks like I committed suicide, get that NCIS guy in here for a closer look."

"Yes, sir, I will. If you'll excuse me, I'm going to sneak my coffee upstairs and get a shower in before I have to run Alex to school," I tell him, raising my mug as I walk past him.

While I didn't make Alex go to school on Monday or Tuesday, I'm following Diane's guidance to be firm with her about returning today. Alex hasn't been thrilled with the idea but sitting around watching TV in a house without WiFi hasn't worn well. I have a full day of meetings: police, funeral home, and a lawyer; none of which I want to handle with Alex in tow.

As it happened, she was waiting for the bathroom when I finished showering, so it started off on the right track. Heading downstairs, I knitted my brows together, trying to place the voice of a man who was speaking to Fred. I couldn't have been happier when I saw Chains standing in the kitchen, accepting a plate from Diane.

"What are you doing here?" I ask him, confused but pleased to see him.

"Where else would I be, at a time like this?" His simple response tightens up my throat, making it impossible to speak. "Sophia sends her love."

"How's my godson?" I ask, accepting my breakfast from Diane and sitting next to my best friend.

"Getting bigger every time I blink. The surgery for his trigger thumb is today, so Sophia will be checking in with me in a bit," he tells me, making me even more appreciative that he made the journey in spite of that. "What can I do to help?"

"Well, I've been worried about the carpeting with all the extra traffic through here," Diane starts on one of her tangents, startling Chains. Even having met her before, he still wasn't prepared for that and I nearly grin when the food he was lifting up, completely misses his mouth. "You can rent one of those carpet steamer contraptions for me."

"He rode up here on his motorcycle, Diane," Fred contributes thoughtfully.

"Then he may need to rent a truck, too. Unless Maggie will loan him her Jeep, I just don't want to see her driving his bike. A man his size is bound to have a big one!"

While Fred merely turns the page of his newspaper, Chains has turned purple and I'm halfway out of my chair when I see that Maggie—who had started to step into the kitchen, has decided she's better off back in her apartment over the garage and far away from this craziness. We have a momentary standoff as I try to re-open the door that leads to the driveway, while she tries to hold it closed.

"Oh no, my love," I laugh, reaching an arm out to pull her inside. "You don't want to miss this."

"But I do," she whispers adamantly, shaking her head.

Diane has continued speaking and when I turn back, it's to Chains asking, "I don't understand what is happening. What's a clucky?"

"Clucky is Gran's friend," Maggie announces, sighing in defeat. "We buy our eggs and veggies from her. Gran, I'll pick up more food today, don't worry about a thing. Chains, it's nice you could be here. I'll handle the carpet steamer, why don't you two make a break for it and I'll get Alex to school?"

I look at her askance, and with her nod, I give her a

hard kiss before I jam a quarter of my waffle into my mouth, and signal to Chains to follow me. "Thanks, everyone!"

"It was like we were on the highway, then all of a sudden it turned into a roller coaster," Chains mumbles and a glance over my shoulder shows that he's directly behind me, looking somewhat shellshocked.

"Dude, you met her a few months ago…"

"It was Christmastime, I figured she'd been hitting the schnapps," he replies, and I laugh.

"Damn, the thought of her on schnapps is terrifying. Diane's sharp as a tack, but you never know what's going to come out of her mouth next," I tell him. "I gotta bunch of shit to get done today, you mind riding along with me?"

"That's why I'm here, brother," he replies, clapping me on the back.

Getting on my bike, I admit to myself how good it made me feel, coming downstairs after my shower to see him here for me. Finding my blood brother, and having the time with him that I have has meant the world to me, but I've missed the man who became my brother through circumstance.

We were barely in first grade when we met on our first day at a group home, but where Chains was lucky enough to be taken in by his uncle, I spent most of my childhood bouncing around foster homes or on an air mattress in his bedroom. We had joined a local MC together when we were barely out of high school and when that turned into a shit storm, we had the opportunity to patch over to the Northern Grizzlies.

While I've happily been a nomad with them for years now, that option came to a screeching halt the moment I found out my brother died, and that Alex needed someone to raise her. No one knows me like Chains does and having barely had time to process Nathan's loss, having him here to help me figure out what my next path will be, means a lot.

"Fuck, tell me we have time for a beer?" Chains pleads with me after we finish the three meetings I had today.

"There'll be some at Nathan's," I tell him, fishing the keys out of the packet that the sheriff gave me. "Diane is willing to get in there and do the cleanup, but I want to walk through it first. Alex has track and will get dropped off by five, so I want to be home by then."

"Getting this dad stuff down, huh?" he asks, nudging me with his shoulder as we approach our bikes.

"Come on, let's go raid his fridge."

Sitting down on the couch sometime later, I just stare at the dried blood on Nathan's favorite chair and know he did not die easily. I want to fuck up that bitch and her boyfriend more than I've ever wanted anything, but me ending up in jail will not help Alex.

It. Will. Not. Help. Alex.

Words I repeat to myself a lot these days. Is that what parents do all day? Ask or tell themselves what's in the best interest of their child? What if I fuck it all up?

Chains had taken one look at the scene, then headed back outside. He finally reenters with a tarp and leaves the door open as he crosses to the chair. "We can load it on the back of his truck today, then take that and whatever else is trashed to the dump tomorrow. I just checked and it closed about twenty minutes ago."

He hastily covers the chair before looking over at me. "It's not an altar, Silver. I doubt this is how or where, he wants to be remembered."

His blunt words shake me out of my reverie, and I stand, crossing to help him wrestle the heavy recliner out of the front door. "The rug next."

"Tell me what you know about the boyfriend, I'll get Wrench on it," he quietly huffs after we get the damn thing up on the truck bed. "Prison's too good for them."

I give him a nod, knowing that words aren't needed between us. Chains wouldn't have any doubt about what I was thinking.

Once we get the rug out of the house, I head to

Alex's bedroom and after seeing all the clothes that she has jammed in the closet, I'm pretty relieved she had enough from her mom's apartment, along with things that Maggie picked up for her. Regardless, I grab the first couple of shirts from the center of the rack, knowing it'll be a couple more days before we return here.

Chains makes a gagging sound before I hear a couple of bottles being opened.

"Looks like he was marinating some meat," he says needlessly. I go for the garbage can before I accept the beer and dump all of the perishable shit from the fridge, putting the garbage out back before I allow myself a drink.

"Looks like I'll have to make a run over to Clucky's before we move in." I crack a grin in his direction, and he flips me off.

"What did the lawyer tell you?" he asks me.

"That Nathan fucking hated lawyers," I answer, not able to help the laugh that comes out of me, remembering the conversation from this afternoon. "But he adored his daughter, so he made an exception and kept his will up to date."

I finish the first beer and go back for seconds. "I'm her guardian and this property will be kept in trust for her."

"Are you going to raise her here?" His voice is much quieter, knowing all the implications of any possible answer I have.

"I'd be too far from the nearest chapter to be any good to them on a daily basis. If I did, Alex would be raised around people that she knows—but who will always look at her and remember what her mother was capable of. And Maggie is here." I list off the pros and cons of the first option before launching into what I've categorized as *the big leap*, in my head. "Or, I tell Alex that we're moving to Idaho. And pray Maggie is open to moving out there. Maybe see about buying that piece of land next door to you and Sophia."

"Were you going to do that before this happened?"

I know he's asking me about Maggie, and I just suck down more beer while I organize my thoughts.

"I don't doubt that you love Maggie. But are you just comfortable with things, and how she's helping with Alex?" His second question is more important than his first as he patiently waits for me to answer. I'd be pissed as hell if anyone else asked me these questions, but they aren't unfair.

"She's nineteen, well, twenty now, and has her whole life ahead of her. Her grandparents are here, but she's not otherwise tied to the area. We had talked about her going on the road with me for a while this summer, to see how she'd like it. That's out of the question now, with Alex to think of. But how do I ask her to come help me raise a kid…" I stop mid-sentence, knowing how completely unfair that is. I love her too much to fuck up her life before it starts.

Chains lets out a bark of laughter before standing up to grab the last two beers in the fridge. "I never expected to see you so tied up over a woman."

"She keeps me on my toes," I respond after another long pause and he snorts, giving me a nod when I make eye contact with him.

"Yeah, that's how I feel about Sophia." Those words may not seem like much, but I'm well aware of the depth of his feelings for his Ol' Lady, and take them as his acknowledgement of how I feel about Maggie. "I've seen Maggie cradle my son, Sam. And click her tongue at Alex when she was being rude. She might not have signed up for a man with a teenager, but she won't run from it either. Unless you push her away."

EIGHT

SILVER

"You sure I can't convince you to move in?" I ask Maggie, biting down on my grin as I enjoy the view of her pale ass as she digs through my laundry basket mumbling to herself.

"Found 'em! And no, it's important for you and Alex to get into a rhythm. Besides, there's no room for all of my equipment here," she says, pulling out a pair of panties, shorts, and a top from the clean clothes that are mostly hers anyway.

"Come here," I demand, tugging her hand to pull her back into bed as soon as she gets close enough. I take a moment to situate her on my lap and grin at how nervous she looks. "Is me raising Alex too much for you? I understand if it is, but we should sort this out now."

Whereas, I've started going to therapy with Alex, on the advice of her teacher, Maggie's stuck with my attempt at relaying what the shrink discusses.

"First of all, most days it seems like Alex is raising you," she hedges, giving me a smile. "And no, it's not too much, I'm just scared of getting too attached, then realizing a few years from now that we're together because you didn't want to hurt my feelings."

"Where the fuck is that coming from?" I shout that louder than I should, then growl and wrap my arms tightly around her, stroking her back. "Maggie, Christ, I feel like I've just been waiting for you to walk away. You and me, we had plans for the summer, you have all these plans for your life and now? Now, I have a teenager I'm responsible for…"

"I understand, as well as you do, how quickly life can veer off track, Silver." She assures me, and considering how she suddenly lost her parents, I know she's not blowing smoke up my ass.

"Three months on the road with you? I had misgivings about that, since we're being honest, but I wanted to experience something you're passionate about. And I figured if we survived that, the rest of our story would just write itself," she says with a smile, soothing the side of my face with her fingers. "Right now, Alex gets priority, once you catch your breath long enough to start making long term decisions and not just reacting to what the day throws at you, we'll have time to talk about us."

And she's right. When I make the call of where we'll live, we can all start planning, rather than waiting for the future to magically take shape.

MAGGIE

I know we're having a serious discussion right now, but between Silver's adamant outburst in response to my fears and the feel of his flesh against mine as I sit on his lap, I get worked up again. Just being in his presence is generally all I need, knowing how he makes my body feel.

Shifting, I bend my left knee to maneuver it between our bodies so I can straddle him. The sudden arch of his eyebrow tells me he knows what I'm thinking, at the same time his velvety cock starts to twitch and harden in approval.

"Babe?" he moans, as I slide my slit up along his length.

"Uh, huh," I gasp against his mouth when his hands settle around my hips, pulling me in against him. I squirm, loving the pressure against my clit.

"I'm too old for you," he tells me, lightly kissing my lips as I continue to rock against his cock.

"Men are notoriously less mature than women, so

we're basically the same age," I inform him, nibbling on this lower lip.

"I have a child to raise." Is the next item on his list, as he tries to warm me off.

"Correction: you have a teenage girl, and I know more about them than you do," I say, tugging on his earlobe.

"That's because you are one," he chuckles, and when he raises a hand to comfort the ear I just assaulted, I break free long enough to finally sheath his cock inside of me. "Or were, a few months ago."

"Stop talking," I demand, leaning forward to kiss him again as I gently slide my pussy up and down his shaft.

I take it as agreement when he deepens our kiss, clasping my head with one hand and my ass with his other, while allowing me to set our pace. I arch my hips, making sure that his cock hits that bundle of nerves inside of me with each movement. When his mouth leaves mine, it trails down to my nipples, careful to give each equal attention.

"Need some help?" he asks, knowing that the closer I get to my orgasm, the harder it is for me to keep the steady rhythm that I need.

I barely catch myself from shrieking, when I suddenly find myself on my back with my ankles over Silver's shoulders. "Harder, Sam," I plead with him, not minding the feeling of being a pretzel when he leans in to kiss me.

Remembering to be quiet is my second failing when I'm nearly coming, but I bite my bottom lip and maintain eye contact with Silver in a silent promise that I won't wake Alex up. Seconds before my climax hits, I feel the warm splash of his release filling me up and I squeeze his cock as hard as I can; until he collapses on top of me.

"I love you, Maggie," he whispers the words in my ear, but it's the worry in his voice that hits my heart. Turning to look him in his eyes, I cup his cheek with my hand, not sure of how to chase away his insecurities.

"I love you, too, and I'm not going anywhere."

"How about to Idaho?" he nervously asks, and I widen my eyes in a silent question. "I'm thinking of moving back there. I can get work there and still be active with the Northern Grizzlies."

"How bad are the winters?" I ask, letting his question sink in for a moment.

"Not as bad as other places," he hedges with a small grin. "Not as good as some."

"Like here."

"Like here," he quickly agrees.

"Have you mentioned it to Alex?"

"No, I wanted to run it by you first. We have to

think about your grandparents, after all," he thoughtfully responds.

"My grandparents are going shopping for an RV today," I inform him. "They seem to want to downsize and keep mentioning how *hot* the market is in town. It's like they're saying: *we're not asking you to move out, but we're selling the house.* In their own way."

"I want to go back for a few weeks and get some things ready," he tells me, letting me know how much thought he's actually put into it. "I found information on an overnight camp not too far from here. It starts a week after school is out, so I'm going to send Alex there to buy me a little time."

"Um...do *we think* Alex is the overnight camp type of girl?" I scrunch my brows together, not sure that I can picture that.

"It'll be good for her. I would have killed for something like that when I was her age." And with that statement, I decide not to try to talk him out of it. Growing up like he did, I know how much he wants to give her the opportunities he didn't have as a kid.

Just then my phone pings, and I sigh, knowing I have to leave, or I'll be late meeting Di. "I'll be back in a few days. We'll talk more then."

"Look, I get that he's super hot, but I need you focused on me. Understand?"

Di's been annoyed with me since I started seeing Silver, and that got worse when I wouldn't get her an interview with Nathan. She nearly stroked out when Nathan was murdered, and I said I would stop working for her if kept trying to get details from me.

"I've got you covered, don't worry," I assure her.

For the next five hours, we film segments at various hotspots around town before she finally gives it a rest. We're supposed to get a few hours to chill before heading out to some new restaurant and then an exclusive club.

More than once during the day, the sound of motorcycles had me looking around, only to see that it was members of the Knights on some sort of pub crawl. I don't know much about them, other than that they and the Northern Grizzlies have some sort of issue.

When we get to the hotel, Di pitches a fit over the room only having one queen bed—even though the poor girl at the front desk insists that's what the reservation specified. After finding out there's a couch in the room, I wave it off; even when the couch turns out to be an overstuffed chair with an ottoman. Putting my bags down next to it, I reach over to pull the comforter off of the bed before burrito-ing myself for a much-needed nap.

I wake to the sound of Di singing in the bathroom as she gets ready for the evening ahead and I wonder how much longer she's going to continue the façade of her so-called Influencer life. When I first started working with her, I would get my own room; although I was never certain whether her dad was paying for it, or as she insisted, the hotels would give her rooms in exchange for reviews.

The past few months, I've actually had to hold onto some of the videos until her payment cleared and she's been much more frugal about where we eat. In other words, I'm glad that Sophia has opened up another revenue stream for me, because I can see the writing on the wall. The work I'm doing for Sophia and other authors she's introduced me to has kept my income fairly steady.

"Maggie, you should start getting dressed," Di announces, popping her head out of the bathroom. "You don't mind coming back here after dinner, do you? There's this guy I've been chatting with online, and I'd like to use my extra pass to get him into the club instead of you."

"Not a problem," I answer, completely relieved that I won't be expected to follow her around all night.

"Great, you can get to work on editing everything from today," she instructs me as she saunters to her suitcase. "I don't want any delays this time. Mick, this guy, has great content on his page and I really want to wow him so we can collaborate on some things."

"Sure, you're paying me tomorrow, right?" I ask her, noticing the way her mouth dips down on each side. I've always been adamant that I be paid with actual money as promises of exposure rarely pay off in my line of work.

"Of course," she says after a moment, but I know her well enough to know her first instinct was to unleash her temper on me.

Later that night, I call Silver as I'm driving home. I find myself relieved that I always held my ground with Di and didn't buy into her hype. I had been fast asleep when she came back with the guy from the club and asked that I hang out in the hotel lobby for an hour or so.

I had already emailed her the invoice for the work I had done all day, so after quickly changing out of my pajamas, I grabbed my bags to hit the road. Seriously. Did she honestly think I was going to hang around in the lobby and leave my equipment behind while she bumped uglies with a rando?

"When are you going to Idaho?" I ask him.

"The second week of June. Does this mean I'll have some company?" His voice sounds hopeful, encouraging me to let out the breath I wasn't aware I was holding.

"I'd like to get a feel for it, but yeah, I want to go with you. If I'm still invited," I tell him.

"Why wouldn't you be? Oh, and I got Alex signed up for camp today. She'll be there for six weeks, so that'll give me time to get everything lined up in Idaho."

"How did she respond?" I ask him.

"I thought we could tell her together," he hedges a bit.

"Oh no. This is an uncle-niece conversation, that uncle's girlfriend will not be a part of," I immediately inform him.

The silence drags on longer than what's comfortable, but I wait him out. "So, you're my girlfriend, huh? And we're going steady?"

"Damn right, we are," I answer with more confidence than I felt when I slipped that label in a moment ago. I know he made me promises months ago, but I haven't been sure how to make sure that we're still on the same page since then.

"Good. Now that I know that's absolutely straight in that brain of yours, no more pussy-footing around! I want you moving in with us ASAP," he demands, and I realize I fell right into his trap.

I can't contain the grin on my face or the reaction my body has when he gets all growly like that. "I'll go home tonight and start packing first thing in the morning."

"Good girl. Text me when you're home." His voice and the chuckle he releases sounds like he's as relieved as I am.

"I love you, Sam," I whisper when we've hung up. In my mind, that's how I think of him, even though I know he prefers his road name. "Sam."

Saying his name again, I decide to start using it more often and not just when we're in bed.

NINE

SILVER

"Couldn't wait to get rid of me the first chance you got, could you?" Alex's sharp voice is not a pleasant way to wake up.

"What the fuck are you talking about?" I ask, looking at the bedside clock and wondering what the hell she's doing up this early on a Sunday.

"Overnight camp? For six weeks! Does any of this ring a bell? I got a welcome email this morning from some woman introducing herself as my counselor for the summer, and I thought it was a joke. Then I saw the pamphlet on the desk. I'm not going!"

I let out a loud sigh. "Give me a minute, Alex, I'll be right out."

When she continues to glare at me, I point at the

door. Alex crosses her arms over her chest to let me know she isn't budging, so I lower the covers and that gets her moving. I have sweatpants on, but apparently, she didn't want to take the chance of seeing me in my boxers.

Emerging fully dressed a few minutes later, I hold up my hand. This conversation will require coffee.

Staring the pot down, I will it to brew faster as I furiously think of what to say.

"When the internet became a thing, I would hang out at this place where I could pay by the hour to use a computer. Most of the kids in there were gaming, but I was searching for Nathan. I didn't know shit about how to do it and this lady would talk to me sometimes, giving me suggestions. Finding my brother was the only thing that mattered to me," I tell her, finally getting some coffee in my mug. "This past year…"

My voice cracks, and I try to cover it by taking another sip, but burn my tongue instead.

"Nathan and I aren't, weren't, big on discussing our feelings, but, finding out that he trusted me enough to update his will and make me your guardian tells me that he felt the same way about me, that I do about him." I turn to face her, relieved that a little of her anger has faded from her eyes. "But I need a minute to figure things out, Alex. That, and when I saw the flyer for the camp, it brought up all these memories, well, it looks freaking awesome."

"Why didn't you ask me if I wanted to go?" she demands, in a much softer voice than she woke me up with.

"I wanted to surprise you. It was actually supposed to be a *good* surprise." I insist.

"Can you get your money back?"

"No," I lie. I might be able to, but I need Alex someplace safe, while I try to figure out our next steps. "And there's something else."

"Boarding school?" She crosses her arms over her chest again as she sneers that comment out. This is usually the point that Nathan would start mumbling about teenage girls, and I'm starting to understand what he meant. Her attitude is a whole lot less funny when it's pointed in my direction.

"I want us to move to Idaho," I throw that little grenade out there and wait for the next explosion. Carefully watching her face when it doesn't come, I cautiously continue. "With Chains, Sophia, and the Northern Grizzlies that I know the best, I can find some decent work and we can start over."

"What about Maggie?" she asks after a moment, turning to look out of the window.

"I'm hoping she'll come with us." I stop myself before mentioning that Maggie agreed to come scope out the area while Alex is at camp.

"What about this place?"

"It's yours, when you turn eighteen. We can have someone keep an eye on things…"

"I don't want it." Her voice sounds strained again.

"That's not a decision we need to make today, honey," I let her know, stepping forward to wrap my arms around her.

"When does Chains get back from Virginia?" Alex asks me next, and I just shrug. Vector needed a *fresh face* to help with a job, and I was lucky that Chains was here and could go in my stead. "And Maggie?"

"Um, well, I think she might be moving in with us today and she'll come to check out Idaho while…"

"While you ship me off to camp," Alex snaps, pushing me away again. "And what if I don't like Idaho?"

"We'll make the best of it, there are tons of things to see and do out west," I tell her, getting a little annoyed at the attitude that's being flipped on and off.

Is my plan perfect? Absolutely not, but it's the best I can do right now and it's not like the average kid gets to pick and choose where they live.

"Like it or not, you're stuck with me until you hit eighteen, kiddo. I hope you'll want to stick around after that, but I have a network in place back there where I can get work and be home for you at night. So, yes, this summer you *are* going to camp while I find a place for us to live and close up this house. Next summer, we'll be more settled and will plan a vacation or something—together. Deal?" I stick my hand out, hoping she'll give up the fight, but knowing it won't be that easy.

Without a word, she turns around and walks to her room, slamming her door.

"Okay, good chat," I mumble, wondering if it could have gone any worse.

"We're going to breakfast in ten minutes," I yell through the door to her room and am answered by blasting music.

Next I call Maggie, asking if she wants to meet us. When she turns me down in favor of packing, I do what any man would.

Beg.

Maggie's presence has the exact effect on Alex that I had hoped for—while I don't mind being the bad guy today, the two of them working together to make Maggie's move go smoothly gives Alex something to do other than sit and fume in her room.

"You drew a pretty hard line with her today," Maggie observes as we're going to bed that night.

"Have I mentioned Angela?" I ask and immediately feel her tense up at hearing another woman's name.

"Is that Chains' cousin?" she asks after thinking it through and I feel her relax again.

"Yeah, his uncle said something once that I've been thinking about a lot lately." I pause, trying to find the words to explain what I'm worried about and what I'm trying to prevent. "He said, 'I always gave up the little fights with her, thinking I would win the big ones, the ones that mattered. But the little ones mattered more than I knew.'."

"What did he mean?" she questions me, looking puzzled.

"After his wife died, he wanted Angela to be happy, so he pretty much gave her free reign. He told her what time he expected her home, but he never enforced it. He told her he didn't want her dressing like a, well, you know. He didn't want to fight though. He didn't want her dating until she was sixteen, and definitely not a drug-dealing biker a decade older than her. When he became a grandfather, much earlier than he planned and she moved out to be with her abusive, dickhead of an old man, all he could do was set up a trust so she would have the house after he passed." I let out a heavy sigh, because although he never acknowledged it, he felt like he lost all of us—Angela, Chains, and me—to the Iron Savages.

"Did she have anything to do with why you and Chains became Northern Grizzlies?"

"I can't talk about that with you, babe," I tell her honestly and although she looks annoyed, she doesn't push it. "I'm not going to try to unilaterally make all of Alex's choices for her, I just need a minute to figure this all out."

"How are you doing?" The tenderness on Maggie's

face relaxes me more than anything else I can imagine, and I grin, motioning her closer with my forefinger.

"I have a very important question for you," I whisper, transferring the small silver cylinder from my hand to press it against her palm. Her cheeks blaze scarlet when she realizes what I had found during the move, but I just grin. "Wanna tell me how anything that fucking small is able to pleasure a woman?"

"It's meant to be discreet!" she nearly shrieks before catching herself. "And, with lack of suitable options, it got the job done."

"And now?" I tease her, rolling her onto her back as I lie beside her.

"Now, you get *the job* done," she answers, her blush fading as she gains confidence.

"I don't know, I may need some pointers from your tiny, tiny friend," I counter, sliding her hand that's still clutching the silver bullet down between her thighs. "Why don't you demonstrate?"

Wiggling until her night shorts give me a little peek of her pussy, she tugs on one of my hands, moving it over her breasts in a silent request for assistance. Just as I start to flick a nipple, I hear a faint buzzing sound, her hand barely moving as she holds the vibrator against her clit.

Discreet is an interesting word, I think later when Maggie is softly snoring next to me. One we'll have to work hard on with a teenager asleep in the next room.

Maybe the home we find in Idaho should have a little more space.

After chasing my tail all morning, I slow down when I see some familiar bikes outside a roadside bar that sits between town and Nathan's land. Pulling up next to them, I text Maggie about picking Alex up after school then head inside.

It's dark inside, taking my eyes a moment to adjust, but a sharp whistle greets me, and I quickly see Chains, Vector, and Roman sitting at a high top just past the bar.

"Anything?" Chains asks when I pull up a chair and flag the bartender for another pitcher.

"Diddly-fucking-squat," I mutter, narrowing my eyes when the guy behind the bar leaves the beer and an extra glass on the bar, rather than walking it over to us.

I open my mouth to say something to him, but Vector shakes his head, waiting until I've retrieved it before continuing. "I told him to give us space."

"I went back to Prim's apartment and talked to some of her neighbors. She owed a few of them money, then her landlord tried to get me to cough up a couple of months' worth of rent. I had already tossed her place by then, as had the cops, so I told him to keep what was left."

"Now why do I think that went over like a turd in a punch bowl?" Roman chuckles.

"Because she doesn't have jackshit to her name," I respond. "She ain't my problem. One of the neighbors said some 'biker thugs' had been there to party a time or two. And that they were an improvement over the 'scummy looking boyfriend'. She seemed like the type who would be watching things through her peephole, but since she was the only one who asked after Alex, I slipped her some cash. Prim's manager at the grocery store didn't have much to say, other than that the cash drawer was no longer light."

"Roman's been following up with some contacts of his," Vector informs me. "They mentioned a new MC trying to muscle into the area west of here. The Corrupt Bastards."

"Ain't many of them from what I've heard, and they've made enough enemies that they don't stay any place too long," Roman clarifies what his contacts told him.

"Do you need to get Alex?" Chains asks me, looking at his phone.

"Maggie's going to take her for a manicure when school lets out today," I let them know. "Y'all can join us for pizza if you're sticking around."

"Listen to you, saying 'y'all'," my lifelong friend

mocks me just as I notice Vector and Roman exchanging a look.

More than a look really, it's like they're having an entire conversation without saying anything out loud, until Vector finally nods. "If we could crash at your place, we'll stay another day or two to see what we can suss out. It wouldn't do to be seen going back and forth too much. If word gets back to Maverick, things could blow up again."

The Satan's Knights MC has a chapter an hour or so east of here, and the Northern Grizzlies know the territory line better than their home addresses.

"You eating grits now, too?" Chains continues, trying to keep the mood light. "Or pineapple on your pizza?"

"That pineapple shit is California, asshole," Roman pipes up, with a shit eating grin stretching across his face. "Maybe up in DC, but not around here."

"This time next year, you'll be eating pineapple on your pizza," Vector predicts, jabbing his elbow into Roman's side.

"Fuck off already," Roman grunts. His eyes shift past his empty glass, and he reaches for the half full pitcher, picking that up and downing the contents.

Now it's my turn to exchange a glance with Chains, and I agree with what I see in his eyes. It's best we stay out of whatever the hell they're going on about.

Chains gets up to order another pitcher, then we get

back to plotting out how to track down Prim's boyfriend before we head out to meet Alex and Maggie.

After dinner, I join Roman for a smoke outside the restaurant. We stand around, shooting the shit until I see him look back inside the restaurant.

"How'd you know?" he asks me. "Has it even been a year since you met?"

"I knew the first time she grinned at me," I answer, grinding out the cigarette with the heel of my boot. "A woman like that and a man like me? Well, I'm smart enough to lock her down."

He nods his head before asking for the key to the gate, letting me know he'll be riding ahead of us.

TEN

ALEX

"Just go already!" I nearly yell at my uncle, before noticing his best friend walking around the parking lot. "And what is Chains doing? Taking pictures of license plates?"

"What? Did you think I was going to leave you here among strangers for weeks without knowing anything about the other families? Alex, I've told you, if you're miserable I'll pick you up in a month," he growls back in a near whisper, swiping his hand through his hair and looking appropriately worried about leaving me in this hell hole of bareboned wooden structures and all sorts of activities that seem set on killing the weak links.

Hmph. Maybe I can have some fun after all.

"This is so embarrassing," I moan. "Look, I'll be fine, I'm sure they have electric fences and stuff to keep us all safe."

The flash of humor in his eyes is the only warning I get as Silver looks momentarily confused before tilting his head. "I think the brochure said those are just around the swimming area."

"Maybe if I touch it, I'll get a matching silver streak in my hair like you and Dad!" I break eye contact with him the moment those words are out of my mouth and wish I could take them back. I can't seem to stop myself from mentioning Dad like he's still alive and it just keeps making Silver and me feel bad.

"I'd hug you good-bye, but then the other kids wouldn't think I was cool anymore," my uncle's voice is softer when he deadpans that, and I'm relieved I didn't totally ruin the moment.

"How long have you been working on that line?" I sass back, happy that our normal give-and-take has survived The Murder.

He leans down and right before I think he's going to kiss my cheek like Dad used to, he whispers, "I snuck a burner phone into your bag, leave it turned off because you won't be able to charge it, but call me if you need to talk."

"I love you," I whisper back, really meaning it. Phones top the list of 'contraband', but just knowing that I have a way to reach him if I need to, reinforces his earlier words: that he doesn't feel trapped by having to care for me now.

"Me too, kiddo." He takes a moment before responding, searching my face to confirm my words. I know the man has trust issues, but Jesus, I'm fourteen now, I don't go throwing those words around unless I mean them.

With that he walks away and meets up with Chains near my dad's truck.

Camp wouldn't be too awful, if it weren't for the other kids here.

Christ, they're everywhere. I cross my arms over my chest and sneer at them while I wait for them all to get their canoes. The other day I got mixed up over what activity I was supposed to be at and ended up with just a counselor, rather than crammed into this sad excuse for a boat with four kids who are dying to *accidently* tip it.

"Hey, do you want to share a canoe with me?" a boy, who's probably about my age, asks me. I've seen him at some of the activities and really just noticed him because, like me, he usually hangs back rather than rushing into the group who's always trying to be first for everything.

"What is that? Like a lame-ass pick up line?" I spit back at him.

"Suit yourself. You can spend the hour getting tipped, but I was going to sneak over to the smaller branch of the river and see what's over there." He keeps his voice low and even before turning to walk away.

I look back at the group that's laughing and taking forever to jam their friends into these hot cylinders of torture. "Wait up," I call out and quickly follow to the canoe at the far end.

He doesn't smile or anything as he holds it for me, letting me get in first then move up to the seat in the front. As soon as my butt is on the near-burning metal seat, he pushes it off from the shore and sits in the back seat, without waiting for anyone to join us.

"No tipping," I growl in my best impersonation of my dad, stopping short of threatening to drown him.

"Agreed," he immediately pipes up. "Or I'll leave you to swim back."

As I stare down the river, a small smile stretches across my face. Probably the first genuine one I've had since *the murder*. A counselor calls out after us, reminding us to turn back when we make it to the second marker, which is hanging from a tree well past where our side trip will take us.

"What's your name?" I call over my shoulder, after realizing I don't have any idea who he is.

"Connor. What's yours?"

"You talk funny," I say instead.

"You talk like a red neck, but I haven't said anything about it, have I?"

"Alex." Hmm, Connor may have a funny accent, but he speaks smart-ass just fine.

He quirks an eyebrow. "Was that painful?"

"Excruciating," I fire back.

The corners of his mouth curl slightly, but he catches himself. "And I don't talk funny. I'm from New York. R's are optional, and every word ends with a vowel."

"I live about an hour from here." I volunteer when he stops talking. "Well, I was. After camp, we're going to move to Idaho."

"That's random," he says after a moment. "The turnoff is right up there on the right, let's stay close to the shore for a bit and hopefully no one will notice."

He no sooner says that than we hear splashing and screams behind us. I turn to see him grinning before I look past him in time to see a second boat tipping over, that should distract the counselors for a while. "No one will notice now!"

"Scared of getting into trouble?" he challenges me.

"I'm not scared," I say defiantly. "But you haven't convinced me you know how to control this thing and I prefer not to end up getting wet after all this."

"It's a canoe not a spaceship. What's to control?"

Silence stretches between us, then I give in and sigh.

"Fine. I guess you're not a people person."

He shrugs. "Depends on the people and *these* people aren't really my kind."

That sparks my interest. "Oh, what's your *kind*?"

"I don't know. Everyone here has a stick up their ass and…" His words trail as he narrows his eyes. "… they all seem to think I talk funny."

A giggle slips past my lips. "So, I'm not the only one."

He rolls his eyes. "No, but you're the only one I don't want to punch for saying it."

The smaller branch of the river is shallower, causing the bottom of the boat to scrape against rocks in some spots. I nearly shriek the first time it happens, wondering how we'd explain destroying a canoe. When that got a laugh out of Connor, I kept my lips smushed together so I wouldn't do that again. Damn if I want some northerner acting more comfortable in the country than I am.

"Stop!" I call back to him when the river turns, opening up to a small lake with a house set on the bank across from us.

"There's not exactly brakes on this thing!" he yells back. His eyes catch onto the house and widen like we've just discovered hidden treasure or something. "Oh, wow! Do you think anyone's there?"

"No, the windows are all shuttered," I reply after studying it for a minute.

"This is really cool," he sounds excited and when I look back to see him taking in the area with wide eyes. "If I knew how to dock this thing, I'd say we should check it out."

"The house?"

"Yeah. Why not?"

"Um…trespassing."

He rolls his eyes again. "It's only trespassing if we get caught."

"Not sure I'm willing to take that risk." Carefully holding the sides of the canoe, I turn to face him and pull my paddle up, laying it across the space in front of me. "We can just stay here for a little while, if you want to."

"Fine." He scratches the back of his neck. "It's for the best. Archery's my next activity and I actually like that."

"I have it right after breakfast. At home, I have my own bow, but I wasn't allowed to bring it with me," I respond, shrugging my shoulder like it's no big deal and happy when he grins at me. "My dad would take me hunting with him."

"The targets here have to be boring after that," he speculates, and I nod my head.

"My dad got me zombie targets when I was

learning how to shoot my rifle." I slide that line in there to impress him and it looks like it's working.

"We don't do any of that in the city. My dad says he will take me to the range out in Jersey when I turn sixteen, but until then it's paintball guns for me. It's total bullshit."

Too soon, we start rowing back toward camp and when we get to the larger section of the river, we can hear the other campers further downstream. From the sounds of it, they gave up paddling in favor of swimming, but we just go to return the boat, checking in before parting for our next activities.

Connor sits next to me at dinner and later at the bonfire. I'm still not thrilled to be here, but having one friend is kind of nice. It's later that week after we've both settled in, that I'm reminded that life is not normal anymore.

I had noticed one of the girls had been trying harder and harder to get his attention and it was one night during free time that she decided that getting me out of the way would clear the way for her. Just as soon as Sheila and her friend, Tracy, moved to sit near me, I knew something was up.

"What about your family, Alex?" Tracy asked me, giving me the sweetest, most innocent look she could manage. "You never talk about them."

"Hush, Tracy," Sheila mock whispers, sliding her

eyes my way. "The counselors said we aren't supposed to talk about *it*."

"Talk about what?" some random boy asks, only tuning in during that last bit.

By now I've frozen, I don't know what to say and I can't seem to get my body to move even though my brain is screaming at me to run. Connor catches my attention and the second I see the pity in his eyes, I feel like I'm looking at him through a tunnel.

Does he know? Has he known all along? How did people find out? The stupid no phone or internet access rule was one of the main reasons I even agreed to come here.

"Now I have to know," Tracy leans in closer to me and the look in her eyes tells me she knows about my dad's murder.

"Fuck off," I tell them, finally able to stand up. "All of you can just fuck off."

"Oh, you better be careful, Tracy," Sheila laughs. "Her mother murdered her father. You don't know what she might do to you."

"Oh, my God, is it even safe for her to be around us?"

I turn and run, trying to get away before my tears start to fall. There's nothing so frustrating as crying when you get angry, but I can't help that now.

"Alex, wait." A quick look over my shoulder shows

me that Connor's catching up and in the relative cover of trees around us, I turn on him.

"Did you know? Is that why you were *nice* to poor little old me?"

"No! Look, I was walking to an activity with them a couple of days ago and we overheard the counselors talking about it. One was worried about you because you keep to yourself so much and the other one told her the story, I guess she lives close to you or something." His words come out so quickly, I can tell he's being honest. Reaching up, I swat at the tears on my cheeks, happy that he's ignoring them; or at least he would have, if a deep shuddering breath hadn't welled out of me just then. "I knew you weren't like them though, that you had, maybe, been through something bad."

"Is that marked on my forehead or something now?" I ask, turning to continue to my cabin on the girls' side of camp.

"Come on, I can't get caught in that section," he calls out after me.

"I know," I choke out, unable to hold back my tears any longer.

Getting to my cabin, I burrow under my blanket and momentarily think about calling Silver. Even though it's just part of my inner monologue, I shake my head. I can't expect him to come running every time someone hurts my feelings. If he's even in this damn state.

Instead, I come up with a new plan and get up to prepare while I'm still alone.

Gradually, my bunkmates filter in and the counselor does her customary head count before silence finally falls over the camp for the night.

I wait for what seems like days, but it's probably only been an hour before I slowly crawl out of my bed and head to the bathroom. The cabins are set up in a square with space for ten girls in each one, with every four cabins connecting to a central building that has showers and toilets.

Since the camp isn't full this summer, the fourth cabin sits empty. After grabbing the backpack I had stashed in the bathroom, I continue through to the empty cabin where I don't have to worry about a counselor sleeping right next to the door.

My escape turns out to be even easier than I thought it would be, I think, as I dart to the wooded area just beyond and check the area for anyone who might be watching. Since I don't think anyone has noticed my escape, I take the path that will lead down to the river.

Getting down to the racks that the canoes are stored on, I notice that one is missing.

"I have it ready to go." Connor's voice scares the shit out of me.

"What are you doing here?" I ask, trying to keep my voice low as I turn to face him.

"W.W.A.D?" He gives me that cocksure grin of his that makes him look older than he is.

"Funny."

"Yeah, it took me like five seconds to figure out you'd make a break for it tonight, so I swiped supplies from the canteen and loaded up the canoe. Now, let's go before we get busted." He gives me this funny little half-bow and motions his arms down toward the canoe.

"You don't have to do this," I tell him, not wanting him to get into trouble even though I'm happy that I won't be alone.

"I know, but it'll be like those survival shows where you get dropped in the middle of nowhere and have to find your way back. Do you have any semblance of a plan, by the way?"

"I was thinking about that house we found. I thought if I could get there, in the morning I could get to the road then find my way home," I answer, getting into the canoe and taking my usual seat in the front.

"And when we get caught trespassing?"

"Don't worry, I'll tell them I kidnapped you," I sass back, getting a grunt in return.

"I've heard that before," he whispers and when I turn to look at him, I instinctively know it's not the shadows from the moonlight that darken his features.

After that we row in silence, Connor seems lost in his thoughts and for the life of me, I can't figure out a good way to ask what happened to him.

We've kept our conversations light since we started talking, neither of us over-sharing about our lives away from here and I feel guilty that I've been so involved in my own pity-party that someone I consider to be a friend has been suffering also.

"Thank you," I whisper over my shoulder to him, before the small channel catches my eye. "Oh, the turn off is up here."

"If you need someone to talk to, I won't tell anyone else what you tell me," he says as he guides us onto the smaller river.

"Ditto," I reply before the house comes into view. "Hey, that window wasn't open last time, was it?"

"I don't know. Let's pull the boat up over there then go and check it out," he whispers back.

I know we're probably going to get into trouble at some point, but tonight, being out here with Connor, I'm having the most fun I've had since my world was turned upside down. With a stupid smile plastered on my face, I reach down for my backpack before we continue.

"No, leave it, in case we have to run for it," he tells me. I nod, but still reach into the side pocket for the burner Silver had given me and slide it into the pocket of my shorts.

The light of the moon reflecting off of the water makes it easy to see our path, but I still follow close behind Connor—nearly colliding with him when he suddenly stops.

"Quick! Into the bushes," he hisses, grabbing my hand to pull me after him.

The scream I was about to release when he suddenly yanked my arm, dies in my throat when I hear people walking toward us. I hurry to keep up with him and when he dives behind some bushes, I land in a heap next to him.

"So much for it being abandoned," I murmur, but give him a quick nod when he holds a finger over his lips.

Following his eyes, I look to see that the end of our canoe is visible from where we're hiding, which means that anyone along the rocky shore will be able to see it. The anger in the men's voices is loud and clear, even before we can see them. It's when we do see them that I instinctively start to get to my feet, and I would have if Connor hadn't grabbed me again; one hand on my shoulder, his other covering my mouth.

My mom's boyfriend is shoved forward, and for a split second it looks like CJ will try to make a break for it. From the looks of things, he's taken quite a beating already so maybe that's why he doesn't try anything.

"Look, I'm telling you I can get you this girl. Her uncle's patched in with the Northern Grizzlies." CJ murdered my dad and now he is offering me to…the light isn't good enough to make out the wording on the cuts the other three men are wearing, but they're definitely in another MC.

I reach up, squeezing Connor's wrist to silently let him know that I won't make a noise.

"Too late, asshole," a tall man with a shaved-head spits out. "You promised us a contact inside the Knights' clubhouse."

"Yeah, yeah, it's just that my cousin, she was hanging around with them, but she OD'd, so I gotta find someone else." CJ's breathing is almost as loud as his voice at this point and if they weren't about to kill him, I'd be happy to finish him off. "Man, look, I can get you this teenage girl and some money. Prim was sure that her ex had a shit ton of cash hidden at his house. If we can get the girl away from there, her uncle will be searching for her, and I can get in to find the money. Bing, bang, boom—I'll split it with y'all and you can keep the girl."

"Sounds like he's asking us for another favor," the burliest of the bunch snarls, pausing to release a stream of tobacco spit in CJ's direction. "Ain't that the little bitch that's the witness against you and your ol' lady? Fuck this talking, where's this hole we're looking for?"

"Follow me, there was always a sinkhole, up over on this side," one of the men says, looking around to get his bearings.

Naturally, they turn in our direction and for the first time it occurs to me that we should have been slowly backing up, instead of being rooted in place.

"Fuck," Connor releases the word with his next breath, undoubtedly coming to the same conclusion at the same time I did.

"What are you doing here?" CJ asks, taking a step toward us.

"Enough!" Shaved Head reaches out, catching CJ's ponytail, pulling it backward and slicing his throat open before I even see the knife. He wipes the bloody blade on CJ's shirt, then releases his body. Suddenly, he's pointing in our direction. "Shit. Grab them, get them in the cage."

"Run!" Connor and I yell at the same time, narrowly avoiding tripping over each other when we turn to run deeper into the woods.

I don't know when he took my hand, I'm just certain he would have been able to get away if he hadn't been holding it. One of the men tackles me, which pulls Connor down.

Connor is quick to launch himself at the burly guy, punching and kicking him while I worm my way out from under him, gasping for breath.

One noise is startlingly clear, and that's of a gun being cocked before one of the men speaks. "As much fun as it is, watching Cutter getting his ass kicked by a kid who hasn't hit puberty yet, we ain't got the time."

Looking over my shoulder, I see the shaved head guy standing right behind the man with the gun. The burly guy is on the ground, and I can just make out the name on the cut: Corrupt Bastards MC. I've never heard of them, but that doesn't mean much.

"Get walking. Now," the man snarls at us, motioning us past them and back to the house.

I slowly slide my hand down, wanting to pull my phone out even though I doubt that the cops could get to us in time, but my stomach fills with dread when I realize it's no longer in my pocket.

Crap! I carefully scan the ground, looking for any sign of it, but I get shoved for my trouble.

"Hey! Don't touch her!" Connor yells and quickly gets cuffed upside his head.

"Quiet," one of the men mutters. "Christ, what the fuck are we going to do with them?"

"Do you know who my father is?" Connor's words cause my jaw to drop. I can't imagine why he'd think that's going to help us right now. "He wiped the ground with your kind in Massachusetts and he's sure as hell going to do it here if anything happens to us."

"I told you to…"

"Wait, this should be good," Shaved Head says, cutting off the guy with the gun. "Who's your daddy?"

"Bishop from the Satan's Knights." Connor has stopped walking and squared his shoulders as he stares up at Shaved Head without blinking.

I watch the scene in silent terror, convinced he's about to get his throat slit like CJ did. This time when Shaved Head lifts his blade, he brings the flat end of the handle down on Connor's head. Connor sways for a split second before he drops like a rock.

"Cutter, get the kids in the cage," Shaved Head's voice holds no room for argument before turning to the guy with the gun. "You, get rid of that canoe."

"What do you want to do with the body?" Cutter asks him, spitting another long stream of tobacco slime out and making me wish he had choked to death on it when Connor was kicking him.

Shaved Head stares down at CJ's corpse like he forgot he was there, then he simply shrugs. "Fuck it. Leave him where he lays."

ELEVEN

SILVER

A couple of days after I dropped Alex off at camp, Maggie and I struck out for Idaho. She had a whole list of cheesy tourist traps she wanted to stop at on the way. Well, I call them that, she calls them 'true Americana'.

The other Ol' Ladies immediately welcomed her, having heard about her from Sophia and after a handful of days, she was more than happy to start looking at homes we could rent.

"Shit, I gotta take this," I say, seeing Carter's number come up on my phone, and wonder what the retired sheriff has to tell me now. I cross to the door of Jasper's office and accept the call. "Go."

"Mr. Rawlings, I'm the last person you want to hear

from right now, but an old friend of mine told me they are scrambling anyone with a badge at a kids' camp about an hour from here. They seem to be missing two campers and when Barnie, down at the diner, asked me if it was that place you had sent your niece to, I got worried."

A knot instantly forms in my stomach and every instinct I have is screaming that Alex took off. I know she didn't want to go, but I had hoped she would have called me if things got bad. I hold the cell away from my head to check the time, it's not even six in the morning here, adding a couple of hours to that for the time change, I realize the camp is probably scrambling like hell, but if they've had time to call the police, I should have gotten a call by now.

"I'll call the camp, can you please…"

"I've got calls in myself, if I don't hear anything in the next half hour, I'll start driving that way," Carter tells me.

"Appreciate it. Do you happen to know if the Dennisons have left town?"

"They did, a few days ago," he responds, and I let out a grunt of frustration before hanging up. I immediately dial the number for the burner I had left with Alex, but it goes straight to a computer-generated voice telling me that the user doesn't have voicemail.

"Jasper, my niece might be in trouble, I need to get back east," I announce, barging back into his office and immediately getting concerned looks from him, Russian, and Flint.

"What do you need?" Russian asks, reaching for his cell phone.

"A flight," I tell him, since there's no time to waste.

"We're close enough in size, there's a go-bag in my office. Grab that and head to the airport, it'll be handled," he assures me, as Flint excuses himself.

"I'll call Vector to have someone pick you up in North Carolina," Jasper chimes in, picking his own phone up.

On the way to grab Russian's go-bag, I dial the camp and get some fucking runaround that they were just going to notify me and that '*these things are usually resolved within an hour or so*' with the guardians being notified after the campers are found. After having my gut instinct confirmed, I text Chains to let him know I'm flying back.

The harder conversation will be with Maggie, so I call her. Having heard that Sophia and Chains' son had a follow-up appointment with the hand specialist, she convinced Sophia to make it an overnight trip since she wanted to see what Boise had to offer. Unfortunately, that means she won't get back in time to travel with me.

"I was just thinking of you," she whispers over the line when she accepts the call.

"One of these days, I'm going to have time to ask

you what's going through that mind of yours when you say that, but today..."

"Oh God, what happened? I can hear it in your voice." She interrupts me.

"I have to fly back to North Carolina, I don't have any details, but I think Alex ran away from camp."

"Shit, I can come with you," Maggie instantly says.

"No, look, you stay with Sophia and Josh. If I haven't called you by tonight, get in touch with Russian and he can help you with travel arrangements. I'm hoping this is just a wild goose chase," I tell her, trying to keep things light regardless of the feeling of impending doom. "I love you, but I got to get to the airport, okay?"

"Love you too," she says as I hang up before getting on my bike.

While I found it weird that Flint left so fast after I broke the news, that became understandable when he appeared on the tarmac near the small plane a handful of minutes after I did. Then I let out a sigh of relief when Chains shows up and the door is finally closed.

"Jessup will get us there, but he can't stick around," Flint's voice sounds metallic over the headsets we are all wearing. While I'd seen Jessup on one of the weekend rides, I had never actually spoken to the lawyer before today.

"I have to be in court tomorrow afternoon, otherwise I'd stay to help out as needed," he says apologetically. "I've heard a little of what you've been through and I'm sorry for your troubles."

I nod at him, just happy that he was able to get us in the air so quickly. While I never bothered spending time with any of the guys who like to join us on the occasional ride, I realized I needed to check that attitude going forward. Here he is dropping everything to help me out, when I was too self-involved to even nod at him before today.

"Is this a bad time to mentioned that I'm armed?" Chains pipes up, pulling a box of ammo out of his bag.

"Jesus," Flint growls. "We're more than likely flying commercial on the way home."

"Russian just told me to look for Jessup's plane, so I didn't think it'd be a problem." He shrugs before leaning forward to tap the pilot on the shoulder. "You good if I just leave it with you, man?"

"Only if it has never been used in commission of any crime," Flint immediately states, sounding every bit as knowledgeable about the law as the man next to me. "We need to protect Jessup's standing with the Bar."

"Nah, it's clean. It's one of Sophia's."

"There's a bag behind you, if you could please put it in there then stow it under your seat," Jessup instructs him, sounding more resigned than happy. "Either you or your Ol' Lady can pick it up from my office when it's convenient."

The frustrating part about our flying arrangement is the lack of updates. With nothing to be done, I finally put my head back and close my eyes. Chasing sleep is impossible with so many thoughts racing through my mind.

Why the fuck did I send Alex to camp?

Why the hell did Nathan think I could handle raising his daughter?

I've never wanted to kill anyone as much as I want to end Prim.

I've never felt so hopeless in my entire life.

And the hits just keep on coming.

As we are about to land, my phone lights up with messages that came in from cops, camp officials, and Vector over the past few hours. Each one gets my stomach churning harder and harder…

Alex is indeed one of the two missing kids. This message is tinged with hopefulness, considering that the other kid that's missing is a boy that she's 'friendly with'. That statement does not set me at ease, as it occurs to me that everyone's treating this like two kids who snuck off to fuck around.

Especially when I hear the last message, somehow, it's from Vector and not the cops: in their search for

Alex and the boy, the authorities discovered a dead body.

"Easy, Silver," Flint's voice is low and controlled when I look for something to hit.

"I shouldn't have fucking…"

"Sam, you made a call. There's no way you could have known something like this would happen," Chains cuts me off just as Jessup points to an SUV waiting near the hanger he's taxiing toward.

"Looks like that's your next ride," he says, and I see Roman get out of the vehicle.

"You good here?" Flint asks him.

"Yep, I'm going to gas up and turn it around so I can get back without breaking any flight regulations," our pilot responds, and I turn to shake his hand.

"I owe you." Although he shrugs it off like it's nothing, he looks genuinely pleased to have helped me out.

Crossing between the small plane and where Roman parked is the only chance we have to stretch our legs, and if not for Flint, I wouldn't have considered a bathroom break.

"Stopped and picked up some sandwiches for y'all, we're still an hour from the camp," Roman says as we're climbing into his SUV ten minutes later. "Vector and them will meet us there. The men riding through Winston would have been too much of a red flag to any friends of the Knights."

Other than calling Carter to check in, we ride in tense silence until Roman takes the exit for the camp.

"I appreciate this, Roman," I tell him. "If you can't stick around, we'll figure something out."

I don't know the details, but I know we're too close to the Satan's Knights' territory for his liking; not that it stops any of us from wearing our cuts.

"Check it, Vector and the others beat us here," Roman says, nodding at the all the bikes that are parked near, what must be every cop car in the state.

"What the fuck are they doing standing around?" I mumble the question more to myself.

My stomach drops as we walk toward the main building, and while I have no idea where the campers are, there's a whole bunch of anxious looking cops.

Looking to see what their attention is focused on, I see a man getting in Oak's face and ball my fists in rage. We do not need this shit today.

"Fuck that, we're here for your niece. She takes precedence," Flint says, his stride unfaltering as he walks toward the group.

That's when I see a man in a Satan's Knights cut get between them, saying something I can't make out before Vector takes another step forward.

"You motherfuckers the reason that Silver's niece is missing?" Between Vector's tone and his body language, I'd guess we're about two seconds from a punch being thrown, so I pick up my pace.

"Who the fuck is Silver?" the man in street clothes asks him and while I might not know him, I've been around enough clubs to recognize someone with *rank*, when I see them.

"Maverick still trying to fill his daddy's shoes? Evening scores and avenging old debts?" Oak sneers back, swinging his leg over his bike, to tower over the others. Between his size and his shoulder-length blonde hair, wild from the ride, his road name seems redundant.

"This ain't Maverick's beef. Now, I don't know who the fuck you are or who Silver is, but I'm guessing we're all here for the same fucking reason. Two kids are missing. One of them is ours, and one is yours," one of the Knights say before being surrounded by a group of Northern Grizzlies, they're already riled up, and this unexpected reunion isn't helping.

As a group, my brothers seem certain that their enemy holds the key to Alex's disappearance.

"My fucking son is gone too. You want to sit here and point fucking fingers? How do you know your girl isn't the reason they're gone?" The man in street clothes shouts over the others.

"Well, well, what do we have here?" the Sheriff's voice rings out as he makes his way between us and the Satan's Knights. He takes a moment to eyeball the name on each cut. "Been a long time since I seen the likes of you folks breathing the same air as one another.

Someone want to explain to me why a member of the Satan's Knights is here, at the scene of two missing teens—one of them being the niece of a Northern Grizzly?"

"Conner is my son," comes his reply, and I train my eyes on him as I join the group. "I'm a member of the Satan's Knights…the New York charter." He pauses, jutting his thumb toward the one wearing a cut. "Seeing as I'm not from these parts, my brother, here, is helping me out. Giving me and my wife a ride, and a place to land while you fucks find out what the hell happened to my kid."

"You make it a habit of not wearing your colors?" I ask him, drawing everyone's attention.

"I bleed red and black, but my son comes first. Got word my kid was missing, that he was last seen hanging around with a girl that's been dealing with her own trauma and the first thing I did was grab my woman, and my wallet to get us on fucking plane. It's called priorities. Maybe that's why your girl is missing. If you made her a priority—"

I don't give him a chance to finish that sentence, lunging for him, I make the mistake of taking my eyes off the guy in the cut. It's when his fingers wrap around my throat that all my brothers jump into the fray.

We have them outnumbered, but the cops are more than happy to come in swinging and since none of us have the time to take a ride to county, we disengage as quickly as started.

"Enough!" The sheriff barks. "You want to kill each other, go right ahead. I've been itching to put you bastards behind bars for a while now. Be my fucking honor to do it."

His gaze holds each of ours and I turn, giving Vector a nod and he holds up his hands, in almost an apology.

"What I won't do is sit back and have you interfere with official police business. I have a dead body and two children missing. Now, the only people I want to talk to are the legal guardians of the missing children. The rest of you can take your carnage down the road."

Once everyone else has backed off, the sheriff tells us he doesn't know anything yet and turns us over to a deputy who collects our contact information. My eyes meet Bishop's, and I can easily see that his frustration, like mine, solely stems from being sent away without any actual news.

Turning my back on the deputy and Bishop, I turn and head back to where Flint and Vector are standing talking to Sheriff Carter.

"What do we know?" I ask the retired sheriff.

"There were miscommunications about what was happening, so the official search and rescue was delayed," he informs me. The brief shift of his eyes over to where the camp director is talking to the sheriff, her arms waving around, confirms my suspicion that our kids aren't considered a priority. "It seems another camper mocked Alex about, well, the situation with her parents. Then Alex and her friend, Connor, left at some point after lights out."

"And Connor's parents are over there?" Chains asks, nodding his head in the direction of the couple getting into the cage with the Knight who goes by Hawk.

"His dad, at least," I tell him. "She hung back. See what Wrench can find out about them."

"Vector, Chains and I would appreciate it if you could get some bikes for us while we're here," Flint changes the subject, and I know he's not interested in strategizing around anyone with a badge.

Looking at Carter, I thank him and am happy when he takes the hint and heads over to a group of cops standing around talking.

"You good, Silver?" Vector asks.

"Yeah, my brother's bike is back at his place, so I'll be," I answer, getting an annoyed look from him when I purposefully misinterpret his question. "Look, it's a lot of back and forth. It'll get crowded, but anyone who wants to stay can head back to Nathan's with us."

Without any more asinine questions about my feelings, he turns and splits the group up. Half will stay and the others will head home to arrange for loaners for Flint and Chains.

TWELVE

SILVER

Slamming the phone down, I grab my keys desperately wanting to track down the cop I just spoke to and beat the shit out of him.

How can there be no fucking updates? Telling me that the lead detective had an emergency and will call me when he's available?

These are fourteen-year-old kids, with no resources. They aren't on the fucking lam playing Romeo and Juliet.

"Silver," Flint's low voice pulls my attention to where he's sitting at the table, studying a map with some sort of list next to him. He slowly shakes his head, one time, and I understand the message.

Violence will not help right now. I tighten my fist

around the key, not minding the bite of the metal teeth against my palm.

"My ringer is on. I'll be back in a few hours," I tell him, knowing he's trying to keep track of where everyone is.

Pulling out on Nathan's old bike painfully reminds me that I'm failing his memory every second that Alex is gone. I'm not even sure where I'm heading at first, but once I see the sign for the highway, I make up my mind.

The drive to the camp takes a little over an hour and I'm relieved to see that the encampment of cops has cleared out. I can only hope that some of them are working on this case.

Once I figure out where the river is, I follow it up and down, trying each of the driveways until I see the yellow tape that screams 'crime scene'. Leaving the bike near the road, I start walking the property.

It's just past a good-sized bush, not twenty feet from the shore that a glint of metal catches my eye and I reach under a plant to pick up the small flip phone I had left with Alex the day I dropped her off. Hitting the power button, it immediately comes to life, telling me that she didn't have a chance to turn it on before she dropped it.

"What'd you find?"

I spin at the sound of a man's voice and not ten feet away from me is the guy who had his hand wrapped around my throat the day before. As my eyes dart down his cut to confirm his name, Hawk holds his hands in the air as if to say he doesn't mean any harm.

"Alex's phone. With everything she's been through, I hid a burner in her bag in case she needed to talk," I answer him, holding it up. "Has the boy's father heard anything?"

"Nah, the fucking pigs are stuck on the idea it has something to do with our clubs' beef. The Sheriff tailed me after we left the camp, and some of his cronies paid us another visit today, acting like we were responsible for that guy's death." He shakes his head. "They're more concerned with uncovering who killed that low-level dealer than they are with finding out where the kids are," he tells me, before looking over his shoulder. "I was in the house when you walked up, nothing in there stood out to me."

I stare him down, wondering how much I should tell him. How much I even can tell him without pissing off Vector.

"Can we set up a meeting? Your guys and mine, leaving all the bullshit aside for now?" I ask him, hoping this isn't a huge mistake.

"Are you authorized to do that?"

"I don't know. The New Yorker, Bishop, right? I need my niece back and I'm sure he feels the same way about his son, so if you'll give me your word to get the Knights to the table, unarmed, I'll find a way to get the

Northern Grizzlies there." I step forward, holding my hand out.

"Desperate times, desperate measures, I guess," he replies, shaking my hand.

Nodding, I step back to call Vector as Hawk calls someone on his end.

"This is going to be fucking painful," Vector growls after I make my request. "And to top it off, Bridget's on her way down here and she doesn't fucking know."

The second part of his comment is made more to himself than me, but Alex doesn't have time for whatever shit has gone down in the past. I need this alliance to work.

"What the fuck are you talking about?"

"Nadine, my father's Ol' Lady," he tells me, and I nod while holding the phone even though I'm not particularly interested in a history lesson right now. "She was with Preacher first."

"Who the hell is Preacher?" I ask keeping my voice low as I wonder where this is going.

"Was. He was the president of the North Carolina Satan's Knights. His…their…son, Maverick is the current president. And neither him, nor his brother, Shady, have any fucking clue that the three of us share a half-sister," he concludes his family's convoluted genealogy.

"Goddamn it," I say that louder than I meant to and catch Hawk's attention. Striding further away, I lower my voice. "Does this need to be disclosed today?"

"The feud, it was Jigsaw's doing. Nadine was miserable without her boys, and he promised to get them for her," Vector tells me. "If we sit down, I might have to make a concession and it's Bridget who's going to get hurt this time."

My stomach churns at the thought of the havoc Nadine caused, and the ramifications that it might still have.

"I wouldn't ask this if I didn't think it was my best bet to get Alex back," I pause, getting choked up at the thought of what could have already happened to my niece.

"Text me where the meeting will be," he sighs. "There'll be ten Northern Grizzlies there and I'll be pissed if I so much as smell an eleventh Knight in the vicinity."

"Understood," I acknowledge his terms before disconnecting.

"All good?" Hawk asks me when I walk in his direction.

I nod, telling him Vector's terms before getting the location from him.

Once that's settled, at Vector's orders, I ride ahead to scout the barn where the meeting will take place. Now I just have to hope it doesn't spiral into a total shitshow if Vector drops his bomb.

"I don't know how to describe it, but it ain't a barn," I tell the others back at Nathan's cabin later that day.

"Were you in the right place?" Flint asks and while I know I'm exhausted, I keep ahold of my temper.

"Yes. I was in the right place. It is, physically, a barn. But it isn't on the inside," I try to explain to them. "I've never set foot into anything like that before. I was there by myself, and I felt underdressed."

When everyone looks at me like I've lost my mind, I throw my hands up in frustration and start to fish for my phone. A place like that must have a website.

"Girlfriend's back," Bridget calls out from her spot near the window.

We had stopped our planning and spread around to various windows at the sound of a vehicle approaching, so I let out a deep sigh. With Alex missing, some part of me knew Maggie would not be content to stay in Idaho.

Glaring at Flint, he shrugs, letting me know that no one had told him that she was on her way.

The moment I open the door, she wraps her arms around me, only giving me a quick kiss before taking stock of who all's crammed into the cabin. Vector, Roman, Oak, Flint, Chains, and Bridget look at her wordlessly, waiting to see how I'll proceed.

"Maggie, honestly, I don't know how safe it is for you to stay here right now," I tell her. "We have a meeting with another MC, that might or might not make things worse and we still have no idea who has the kids."

"The least I can do is go and open up my grandparents' house," she says after a moment, tilting her head in Bridget's direction. "There's at least one other person here who would like a decent bathroom and clean sheets on *her* bed. I'll keep food at the ready and can help coordinate where people are searching."

"Amen," Bridget whispers. Just a few minutes ago, the finance whiz was advocating for a spreadsheet to track search efforts.

"There *is* something she could do," Flint says, raising an eyebrow in my direction without saying anything else.

I shake my head, wanting to keep Maggie far away from this.

"What?" she asks, prodding us as the silence stretches on.

"No," I firmly respond and feel one of my eyelids twitching.

"I mean, she's the least intimidating of all of us. It's not the worst idea," Chains interjects, to my annoyance.

"Are you going to tell me, or do I need to call the psychic network to find out what you're talking about?" Maggie folds her arms across her chest as she narrows her eyes at me.

"Vector thought it might be helpful to go and talk to Prim. To see if she might have any ideas about who's behind the kidnapping that she wouldn't be willing to share with the cops," I explain the half-baked plan to her.

"That's assuming that Paw Patrol has even gotten around to interviewing her yet," Flint grumbles, getting a chuckle from Chains.

"I'll do it," she immediately responds in a tone that leaves no room for argument.

I know she wants to help—we all want to do something more than sitting around with our thumb up our ass, but considering the number of times Nathan called Prim a *manipulative bitch*, I worry that Maggie's getting in over her head.

"Great, that's settled," Vector says, clapping his hands.

"No, it isn't settled," I counter, turning on him. "Maggie's my…my girl. She and I will discuss this, then we'll give you an answer."

I reach for her hand and tug her gently, so she'll follow me outside without me having to toss her over my shoulder in front of my brothers.

"Is this that growly-possessive thing that Sophia and Riley said I should be expecting you to manifest at any moment?" she asks me when we're out beyond the old stump that Nathan would often sit on in the evenings, and I pinch the bridge of my nose.

"Sweetheart," I start, but seeing the determined look in her eyes, I can tell she's not going to back down. Letting out a sigh, I just kiss her instead.

Pushing her up against a tree, I pour every bit of frustration and feeling of helplessness that I've had since I got the call about my niece into our kiss. Maggie presses down on my shoulders to lift her legs up, wrapping them around my waist as our tongues swirl, fighting for dominance.

The little moan she lets out might sound like she's giving in, but it nearly brings me to my knees.

"Going to prison, even as a visitor, isn't a fucking walk in the park, baby," I tell her, trying to prepare her.

"If I can get even a hint of anything that could help Alex, I will do it, Sam." Her voice is pleading with me, even though she must know she's already won.

"We'll let them know. Then, and I'm serious, I want you to stay away from here in case anyone is watching the property. It's too fucking isolated for you to be here alone, at least at your grandparents' there are neighbors in spitting distance," I insist.

"Aww, you almost sounded Southern, saying it like that!" Mags teases me as we reenter the cabin.

There's no need for an announcement. I can tell from their faces that my surrender was a foregone conclusion.

Vector and Flint sit her down and explain what little we do know, then give her pointers on how to keep Prim talking, in the hope she'll let something slip.

"Besides, from what I've heard about Prim, Maggie's going to do just fine," Flint says, looking confident.

"You think so?" Maggie's eyes search his face for any trace of a lie.

"Sure do, you've got your secret weapon," he replies with this little smirk he usually reserves for when he wipes out his competition at a poker table. Maggie tilts her head and furrows her brow in question. "People underestimate you."

The first real smile of the day breaks across Maggie's face and my heart skips a beat, because Flint said the exact right thing to boost her confidence.

"Prim, for all that she's sitting in there with a murder wrap hanging over her, is going to think she's so much better than you. The Prim's of the world will never understand that glitter-and-a-glue-gun will never hold up to true grit, and you have more than your fair share of the later."

I'll never know, or understand, where the fuck Flint pulled that turn of phrase from, but damn if he didn't peg Maggie perfectly. The eyes of the men around us are all drawn back to her. Even though they've been around her several times, it's like they're seeing her in a new light. And I can't keep the smile from my face—because I've seen it all along.

"Maggie?" I cross to stand beside her, reaching down for her hand.

"Yeah?" she looks up at me with a blush burning across her face, unused to so much attention.

"Will you be my Ol' Lady?" I ask, wishing I had a cut or a ring to give her, anything to mark this moment.

"Hell yeah," she laughs, leaning in to meet me for a kiss as Bridget and the guys cheer us on.

After a quick dinner, I follow the girls and the Northern Grizzlies who've been assigned to watch them back to the Dennison house. I manage to get a little sleep before it's time to ride down for the meeting with the Knights.

Past midnight, ten of us wait in the shadows, near the barn. Once the Knights pass us and there doesn't seem to be any surprises heading up the road, we ride to join them.

Once the introductions are complete, Bishop and I exchange the little that we do know and I start to feel like a temporary partnership might work, until an SUV comes barreling up the road.

THIRTEEN

BRIDGET

The beacon I'm following stops moving and I hit the gas, determined to make it to the meeting in time to find out if it's true.

Every missing puzzle piece of my life fell into place when I overheard Piercer telling one of the prospects that Vector and the others would be fine unarmed. That it wasn't as though he wanted to be responsible for killing my *other half-brothers*. As he explained what he knew to the other guy, I thought my heart would explode.

There's a rage that wells up in me sometimes, it was always the times when it was unprovoked that worried my family the most. My dad would wrap his arms around me—just holding onto me until it subsided.

When I was thirteen and furious at being left out of some activity, I was able to break his hold and run off, that I knew it spooked him. He could beat the shit out of grown men, but his *baby* was strong enough to break free. Not long after that he signed the two of us up for martial arts. It became our thing, and we would practice every day.

Learning to control myself was one of my greatest achievements, but it's times like this that I allow the anger to flow through me.

Today. This moment, I feel more than justified to give license to my rage.

I dial my mom for the third time, and she finally picks up the phone, confused at first due to the hour, but I can tell she understands what I'm asking the moment she says, "Hello?" again.

"Mom?"

"Bridget? Are you still there? There's terrible static..." she says before the line cuts off.

Cursing a blue streak, I start to call her back, but know she damn well won't pick up until she's ready to tell me the truth. Considering she didn't find time to mention it in the last quarter of a century, I wonder if I'll see her this Christmas.

And dammit, she knows I love Christmas.

Seeing how close I am to the tracker, I really hit the gas, and even when everyone turns to look my way, I wait until the last possible second to hit the brakes.

I immediately jump out, slamming the door and looking around.

"What the hell are you doing here?" Vector yells, and I stalk in his direction.

"Why didn't you tell me?" I yell back, quickly nose to nose with the only brother I've ever known. I feel as though I'm looking at our father. "I have to hear about this, *this!* From fucking Piercer?"

"And the meeting location? He spilled that too?" Vector's voice is deceptively low.

His voice gives me pause, knowing what the consequences of *that* would be. "No, the tracker on the bike you loaned Flint told me that. It's from the store and is not supposed to be used for club business."

Seeing the look that Chains and Flint exchange, makes me feel a little bad for not mentioning that fact when Vector ordered the bikes be brought down for them.

I wasn't planning on an audience this size, or anything really, when I set out, but I continue to glare at Vector. He damn well should have told me that I have two more brothers.

"Bridget, we'll talk at home," he growls, and my nostrils flare on their own account.

"Oh, like when I just called Mom and she acted like there was static on the line before she hung up on me?" I tuck my hair behind my ear, and shift my eyes over the crowd, trying to get a clear look at the

Satan's Knights that are gathered, until one of them calls out.

"You want to introduce us, Vector?"

My eyes study the man who asked that, as another man, who's undoubtedly related to him moves to stand beside him.

"I'm his sister, Bridget Morgan."

"We usually call her Fury," Roman contributes, telling them the road name my dad gave me years ago. My eyes flick over to him with the brief promise of retaliation before looking back at the other two.

"Who are you?" I ask the one who spoke. While I don't know their names, I know Vector inside and out. By his body language, I know I'm face to face with my other half-brothers.

The older one takes a step closer to me and I match it, but it's the younger one who speaks up. If I wasn't fit to kill someone, his smile might even be contagious. "I'm Shady, and this is Maverick."

Vector comes to stand beside me. "Nadine is their mother."

At this point, his words are more a promise to level with me, than confirming anything.

"It's good to meet you," Shady says, after waiting a beat for Maverick to speak.

Instead, Maverick looks at Vector before saying, "I think we're done here."

Shady swings his head to glare at his brother. "Mav–"

Maverick cuts him off as he turns and heads for his bike, his final words irrelevant to me. "Silver, when your woman is done with her visit, give us a call."

What the fuck? His indifference burns my blood hot again, until I see the hopeful look on Shady's face. I nod at him before I feel Vector's elbow in my side.

Turning on my heel, he follows me all the way back to my truck before he puts his hand on my shoulder.

"I was ordered not to say anything," Vector's voice is low, ensuring that no one around us hears him explain himself to me. "I've been after Nadine to tell you since Jigsaw died. Instead, she picked up and moved to Florida."

"Knowing you'd never break your word to Dad," I say, filling in the rest. "We'll talk later."

"Love you," he whispers before closing my door.

I know damn good and well that I'm expected to fall into formation with the guys when we head out, so I wait on them. The drive home gives me time to clear my mind, it's when Vector leaves me at Maggie's house without another word that my temper flares again.

FOURTEEN

MAGGIE

I shouldn't have come.

While I was so certain I could pull this off, looking at all the women on the other side of the glass has me promising God I'll go to church every day of my life to keep me away from their fate.

Knowing Alex is all it takes to instantly recognize her mother. Except the closer she gets to me, I see that she's some sort of alter-ego to the girl I know. Hate radiates from every pore of her body as she sinks down in front of me and picks up the phone.

"Who the fuck are you? You don't dress like the other legal aide people," she practically snarls, her gaze dismissing me before she studies the folks in the room behind me.

There are two tiers of prisoners, some get to meet their guests at tables in a big room, others from behind Plexi glass. Considering her crime, it's no wonder she's not allowed in a public area.

"No. I'm not a lawyer. I'm just Maggie." My words trip over themselves and I take a deep breath, knowing I need to get ahold of myself, or she'll walk away. "Um, I'm kind of Alex's aunt, in a way. I'm with her uncle, I mean."

"Oh, I saw him hanging around Nathan's. Enjoy *that* while it lasts, honey." Her mocking laugh clearly shows her disdain for me.

"Look, I'm just here because we're desperate to find Alex and wanted to know if you knew anything about who CJ was mixed up with," I tell her, hoping she cares enough about her daughter to put this other nonsense aside.

"Find Alex?" she asks, with a cruel little smile plastered on her face. "The pigs told me she ran off with some boy. If she's anything like me, she'll turn up in another week. Maybe with a little passenger onboard, if she ain't careful."

"Okay, maybe you don't care that your lover was killed. Whatever," I spit out at her, slamming my hand on the counter in front of me. When the guard looks in my direction, I hold my hands up to show that I'll remain calm. "But the men that left him in the dirt, more than likely have your fourteen-year-old daughter and what do you think they're going to do with her?"

"CJ?" For the first time confusion and hurt wipe away the hate from her gaze and as we stare at each other, it slowly dawns on me no one had told her he was dead. "Are you talking about CJ? CJ's not fucking dead."

I sit back in my seat, nearly forgetting the phone in my hand before I feel the tether of the cord stopping my retreat. This bitch gave zero shits about her child being missing, but she's about to break down over the scumbag that helped her murder Nathan?

Tears start to well up in her eyes, and now the tables have turned as she reads the look of disgust that I don't bother to wipe from my face.

"No. No! They would have told me, someone..." her voice cuts off when she realizes that CJ was hardly the type of guy who had a call-tree organized for this type of situation. "Are you sure?"

"Well, if you didn't know he was dead, you obviously have no idea who he was dealing with and won't be any help." I push away from the counter and act like I'm about to hang up the phone.

"Why do you care? She ain't yours," Prim sneers at me again. It sickens me to look at her, knowing the tears streaking down her face are for her dead lover rather than any true concern for her flesh and blood.

"I'd consider myself the luckiest woman in the

world if I had a daughter like Alex. She's smart, funny, and self-sufficient." With those words, I'm just getting warmed up. Fortunately, I pause to take a breath before I let it slide how much I do care about Alex—the speculative look in Prim's eyes lets me know she's looking for some way to manipulate the situation. "Whatever. Enjoy your life behind bars."

"I'm going to need some money, if you want my help," she quickly says, guessing that I really was about to walk away.

"Do I look like I have money?" I ask, looking down at my clothes from the clearance rack of the local big box store.

"I bet Alex has an idea of where Nathan hid his money, you cut me in on that and I'll tell you where to find the bastards," she tells me, leaning forward as she keeps her voice low. The almost familiar way she refers to the people that are possibly holding her daughter surprises me, but I remember Vector and Flint's lecture and focus on trying to get more hints.

"Nathan wasn't exactly rolling in dough," I say, clicking my tongue at her. "His roof leaks in at least two places."

"Maybe he didn't like banks, but his dad left him plenty, bitch. Everyone always talked about the money those fucking hermits had. All the years they paid for everything in cash and thought no one noticed? Phhf," she bites back, reverting to the haughty façade she had when she first walked out. "Why do you think I got with him in the first place? Unlike that cheap asshole, CJ wasn't averse to spending money to have a good time."

I bite my tongue and try to keep my expression neutral. She's badmouthing the man she murdered because he didn't want to throw his money away, meanwhile, her co-conspirator is dead—probably because he liked to spend more than he had.

Counting to ten for patience doesn't work, so I picture slamming her head against the counter and that is satisfying enough to stay calm as I tilt my head, pretending to care about what she says.

"Anyway, those bastards will find some way to get money for Alex. They have contacts up and down the coast, at least that's what CJ would brag about," she continues talking and my eyes flick over to the sign above the phones, reminding us that our conversation is being monitored.

This is pointless, I think to myself, she's not going to give me anything that she could use to make a deal. Without another word, I hang up the phone and walk to the door, ignoring the obscenities she yells at my back.

When Silver sees me approaching the truck, he slides out of the driver's side, opening his arms so I can walk right into them. My heart is heavy with fear for

Alex and full of love for the man holding me, caressing my back as I gather my thoughts.

"Anything?" he asks after a few moments.

"She knows who probably killed CJ, but she's so damn hateful that she's not going to talk," I mumble into his chest, not wanting to leave the comfort of his arms. "I wanted to strangle her when she said, 'those bastards'll get money for Alex'. Flint might think I'm all gritty, or whatever, but that place is terrifying. And, I mean it's *her* daughter and she won't tell us who might have her!"

"She called them bastards?" Chains clarifies, leaning across the bench seat to be heard through the open door.

I nod my head and warily look up at Silver. I'm about to apologize for wasting our time, but I stop when I see the smile on his face.

"The Bastards are the best lead we've gotten, Maggie," Silver tells me, looking hopeful for the first time. "Chains, text the Knights and Flint. Come on, babe, let's get you home. This is going to be the hard part for you, because I'm going to need you to stay put."

"What am I missing?" I ask, confused at their excitement as I climb into the truck, sliding onto the middle seat in between the guys.

"The Corrupt Bastards are an MC that the Knights nearly destroyed a while back. What's left of them are bottom-feeders, operating between here and Florida, nowadays," Silver informs me, nearly humming with excitement as he pulls out of the lot.

"She referred to the Bastards one other time and I thought it sounded weird, but I didn't know it was another club!" I close my eyes, replaying our conversation. "She's convinced that Nathan has, um, had a bunch of money and said that if we'd cut her in on it, she'd tell us 'where to find the Bastards'."

"She must be pretty confident about their location if she wanted money for it." Chains lets out a whistle. "I'll send that on to the others, the Knights have to have some idea of where the Bastards hole up when they're in the area."

"Prim's apartment was in Greensboro, the Knights are east of Raleigh, and Alex's camp was outside of Winston," Silver says. "I'd guess that would put them closer to Winston-Salem. They wouldn't want to be directly under Maverick's nose."

"And with the Northern Grizzlies west of there, they'd have the perfect alley to travel north or south, since both clubs avoid the other," I fill in the last bit of the geographic puzzle we're working on.

Getting back to the house, Silver walks me to the door and wrings a promise from me that I'll stay put until I hear from him. By now he's programed the retired sheriff's number in my phone and has exchanged a heavy look with Bridget—who's obviously been assigned to babysit me.

"Go away, already!" I laugh at him when he starts double checking the locks on the windows. With a final kiss, he takes off with Chains.

"It never gets any easier," Bridget says from behind me. "I can't tell you how many nights I laid in bed worried my family wouldn't come home to me."

"But you went back to the MC? After college I mean," I ask her, wandering back to see what smells so good in the kitchen. "Did you consider just making a break for it?"

"Of course. It's what my mom wanted for me, especially after Dad died," she replies, shrugging her shoulders. "But Vector and the guys, it's the only life I really know. My brother's different than most, it's unusual to find a woman with as much control as I have. Even if I don't have a seat at the table."

"And now that you've met Maverick and Shady?" I ask, having heard about her recently discovered half-brothers in the Knights. "You don't seem terribly upset with Vector for not telling you about them."

"Oh, Vector and I will be having a longer discussion once this situation is resolved, but I understand how he was raised and that goes a long way toward explaining why he never told me." She grabs a beer from the fridge as I dish up a plate of the pulled chicken that's bubbling in the slow cooker. It's not quite noon, but I sympathize with her needing a drink in light of everything. "Honestly, I'm pissed at Mom. She's the one who should have told me about them. I'm going to hold off on answering her calls until I'm sure I won't lose my shit with her."

I nod with her statement, then the two of us sit there in amicable silence. And I'm reminded of the afternoons I spent with Alex. Sometimes she and I would share a hammock and read our books together. That or sit out on Nathan's 'thinking stump', as she called it as she shared her memories of her dad with me.

Standing up suddenly, I toss my dish in the sink and rush down to my grandparents' bedroom, not wanting Bridget to see my tears.

It's so hard being out of the loop like this, even though I know Silver will contact me the moment there's any news about her. I crawl into the bed, curling into a ball while I dust off prayers I learned long ago.

FIFTEEN

SILVER

Coming up the drive, I couldn't help but smile thinking about how Nathan is either looking up, or down, at us and furious over his front gate being wide open. There's simply no sense in closing it with all the Grizzlies that have been in and out over the past few days.

"Maverick said he has his people out scouting locations," I tell Vector and Flint when I get back to the cabin.

"Yeah, I had to reach out to him," Vector says, without looking away from the map. "A couple of our guys ran into some Knights southwest of here. Temporary truce or not, things are still a bit *tense* between our clubs."

"Rather than running both of our clubs ragged, riding through the same towns, he gave us some locations to check," Flint says. "Roman's cousin owns a bar in Winston-Salem area, so he and Oak rode down there to get the lay of the land from him."

"Sounds good. I'm going to call the detective in charge of the case, then Carter, to see if either have any updates," I let them know, heading out back to make the calls in peace.

After getting re-routed three times when trying to reach the detective, I was finally transferred to a social worker who suggested I head to the station for the most current information. I simply hung up. What was the point in driving an hour to be told the kids haven't been located yet?

"Mr. Rawlings, I had you on my list to call," Carter says, immediately answering when I try him. "I had hoped to speak to an old friend of mine first, but what I have found out is that the deceased was, literally, robbing Peter to pay Paul. He owed a lot of people money, so the detectives are chasing those leads.

"Now, I also heard from a detention officer I know, and I'd like to know why Miss. Dennison paid Alex's mom a visit this morning?"

True to form, Carter just talks until he runs out of oxygen. Considering this is the closest thing to an update that I've received, I stay quiet for another moment–on the outside chance he thinks of something else to tell me.

"Mr. Rawlings?"

"Sorry, Carter, I'm here," I answer him. "Maggie wanted to ask Prim if there was any place her daughter might go *if* she were to run away."

"And she just happened to tell the woman that her accomplice was dead? That doesn't sound like Maggie to me." The tone of Carter's voice lets me know that he's on to me. "You want to tell me what you're planning?"

"No, sir. I don't." Taking a gamble with honesty, draws a rusty sounding chuckle from the older man.

"Considering what you've been through as of late, I'm willing to give you a little leeway. Do not test me, Mr. Rawlings."

Just then, Vector catches my eye so with a promise to check in with him later, I wrap up the call.

"Maverick wants to meet," he says to me, but his eyes are focused elsewhere. "He was trying to relay something without saying it straight out. I don't want to get your hopes up, but they might have a lead on the location for the kids."

I freeze in place. It's like he says, don't get my hopes up, but how can I not? Those kids are living on borrowed time as it is, and the tick of the clock has become my heartbeat. "Let's go. Armed this time."

"Of course. Those cops have anything for you?" he

asks as we reenter through the kitchen, and I reach for extra ammo while we go to meet the others.

I'm not sure where they were all hiding, but including Flint and Chains, there are seven guys out front. "Jack shit," I answer him. "Let's stop and gas up in town."

"Already planned on it," he answers me. "I'm pulling Piercer from Maggie's house. Bridget knows the score and she'll have the prospect there also."

"Vector, where are we heading?" Chains calls out over the various bikes being started up.

"Some coffee house that he knows. Carolina's, down near Burlington. Why the fuck does it matter?"

"If it's anything like that barn of his, I'm not sure I'm dressed appropriately," he answers, getting grins from a few of the guys as we head out.

This time, I do secure the gate.

Social niceties and weapon pat downs are left off the agenda when we join the Knights this time around. My eyes quickly land on Bishop where he stands between Maverick and Parrish, and I stride forward to join them with Vector and Chains at my back.

"What have you heard?" I ask them.

"Did some digging after your text came through,

and it appears the Bastards aren't as dead as we originally thought. Don't have a lot of intel, and not sure how we missed it — that's on me, but from what we were able to uncover, there is a charter out here, and they're housing a couple of bikes with Boston plates. One of my guys is currently tailing one that's been on the move," Maverick says. "He's made a couple of stops, so we're waiting to see where he ends up before we make our move."

"And if he makes your guys? Then what's your plan?" Chains brusquely asks what I was trying to craft into a, slightly, less aggressive question.

"Believe it or not, we have done this before, asshole," Ghost snaps back. Maverick gives him the barest of glances, but he immediately presses his lips shut.

Bishop clears his throat, cutting through the tension.

"He's in a cage. Now if you don't have any more asinine questions, there's some shit you need to know. History that would be relevant if these cocksuckers do indeed have our kids. So why don't you do us all a favor, and take a fucking seat."

Begrudgingly we oblige and Maverick gets right to it, laying all their cards on the table.

"A while back Parrish came to my table in dire need of guns. He had heard I had a deal in place with the Corrupt Bastards, that I was their steady supplier."

One of the Knights grunts but Maverick quickly shoots him a look, silently warning him to keep his mouth shut. "As I was saying, Parrish was desperate, and I thought I could buy some time with the Bastards. We had a good relationship. There was absolutely no reason why they wouldn't grant me an extension, allowing me to deliver what I had on hand to Parrish."

"So, we worked our tails off to transfer the guns. My wife's then husband worked for a trucking company. He tipped us off on a truck carrying a bunch of coffins up North and agreed to move the guns. So, we ripped those motherfucking things apart and concealed all the guns inside the satin liners." I lift an eyebrow at that bit of information, as he continues. "The guns never made it to New York, though."

"What happened?" I ask.

"My vice president at the time was fucking his way through the Sinaloa cartel and he was working with them behind my back to take us all out. He tipped off the Corrupt Bastards, and they intercepted the shipment, killing Colt and taking the guns."

"I'm taking it this Colt fellow was your wife's husband." That guess is confirmed when Maverick's jaw clenches.

"When I learned the truth, that King was playing me, pinning both my charter, and Wolf's against the Bastards, I took action," Maverick shares. "I wear that cocksucker's blood proudly. Once King was out of the picture and the message was sent to the cartel, we rode up North. With Wolf leading the charge, we obliterated the Corrupt Bastards, and took back our guns."

"Left them in ruins," Pipe chimes.

"Do you think that this could be a retaliation for that?" Vector asks.

Maverick considers the question, his gaze shifting between Wolf and Vector.

"It's been too quiet. I mean there were a million opportunities when my daughter was sick for these cunts to strike, and they didn't. Why now? There's something we're missing."

"It could be pure dumb luck, or they could've been biding their time. If you left them in ruins as you say, takes time to build something out of nothing," I reply, shrugging my shoulders before looking back to Bishop. "Does your boy know any of this?"

Bishop looks away, his nostrils flaring as jaw clenches. "It's possible," he grinds out before slowly bringing his eyes back to me. "Can try to shield them from our lives but it never seems to work, does it?"

"You better pray your boy don't have loose lips," Flint growls from across the table. "You did teach him how to keep his mouth shut, right?"

Vector scoffs from beside him. "Would you keep your mouth shut if you were a fourteen-year-old boy with no clue how else to protect the girl you're with?"

Bishop's face darkens with anger at Flint's words,

so Vector's immediate defense of Connor helps ease the tension that they had inflamed.

I take Flint's silence for what it is. Acknowledgement that teenage boys aren't known for much in the commonsense department.

I clear my throat, regaining their attention so I can ask what the plan is.

"Well, we wait for Ink to call. See where this one Bastard ends up. Who knows maybe he leads us to the kids."

"And if he doesn't? We're running out of time here." I needlessly remind them.

"Then we take him for a ride. Bastards squeal like little pigs when they're out in the country with nothing but the promise of wildlife looking to make a meal out of them," Maverick says confidently. "We'll get him talking."

"So, a typical date night?" I smirk back at him and finally see a flash of humor in his eyes. The first tell that the man before me has any emotions.

Suddenly, Maverick's phone rings. He reaches into his cut to retrieve it, and when he catches a glimpse of who's calling, he lifts his chin and stares across the table at Silver.

"Speak of the Devil, and the Devil shall appear." His thumb swipes across the screen, and he lifts the phone to his ear. "Talk to me, Ink. What do you got?"

We all stare at him as he listens to whatever Ink is

telling him. Occasionally he nods, but other than that, he remains quiet.

"Oh, for fuck's sake," Parrish growls. "What's he saying?"

Maverick's gaze snaps to him for a brief second, before he turns and locks eyes with Bishop. "Ink's got eyes on your boy."

I push up out of my chair, bracing my hands against the table as I lean over it.

"What about Alex? Is she with him?"

Maverick nods. "There's a girl with him and they appear unharmed."

Letting out a deep breath, and my eyes flit to Bishop. He looks every bit as tense as he did before that news, since we aren't home free yet.

Maverick wraps up the call and briefs us. When he stops talking, we all head out to our bikes. I look over and can clearly see the wheels turning in Vector's head before he calls out to all of us.

"Phones off, and sim cards out if you have them."

"Hold up," Ghost shouts as he shuts down his bike and removes his helmet from his head, he points between Bishop and me. "Give me your phones. Bash, you stay here with the phones, just in case that piece of shit Sheriff is tracking them, and we need to prove their whereabouts later on."

"Good thinking," I agree, dropping my phone into Ghost's palm. Bash doesn't look thrilled about staying behind, but it is what it is. Maverick shares the location, and we finally get on the road.

I'm certain that Bishop, like me, is itching to push our bike's limits, but with as much hardware as we're all carrying, that does no one any good.

In an effort to avoid cameras, we stay off the interstate and every time the posted speed dips, so does my heart rate. I understand, probably better than most, what could have happened to Alex in the past few days, but all I can hold onto now are the few short words that Maverick gave me; confirming that she's alive.

Nothing else matters.

The Knights have been leading the way, but as they pull up to Ink's truck, they clear a path for me, knowing damn well that I get front row tickets to whatever's about to go down. Vector, Chains, and Flint have my back as we pull into an empty lot for some abandoned factory.

There are signs on every corner, advertising an upcoming subdivision and community center. The problem being, the date listed passed by over a year ago. This area is dead, and it'll be a while before it comes back to life.

"The house is up a block," Maverick informs us as his man slides out of the cage. "Ink's found a way into the basement."

Sticking to the shadows, we set out in two teams

with Bishop, Mav, Hawk, Chains, and me breaking off with Ink around the side of the house, while the others surround it.

I can only guess that this neighborhood was originally dependent on the old factory, but now, except for a few remaining homes that have light shining from the windows, the rest are boarded up. Making this the perfect area for squatters and other vermin, like the Bastards.

As we near the boarded-up window, Ink holds his hand up for silence, then quickly signals the room that the kids are being held in and indicates that there are six others in the front room. He seems to have previously pried the board off a window to the raised basement, and while it'll be tight, none of us are too big to fit through it.

Having been here for a while, Ink seems to be itching for action. Going in, feet first, he lowers himself inside and we all hear the slosh of water when his boots hit the floor. Dammit, that's going to make things interesting.

Scanning the basement with a small tactical flashlight, he waits until we're all inside before he shines the light on the path to the stairs. The cheap, wet carpet continues across the room, and I know we'll need to step carefully to make it across without alerting the men upstairs.

The sound of their muffled argument becomes

clearer the closer we get to the old wood stairs. When we make it to the lowest step, Ink looks around at each of us and with a nod to Chains, he motions him to head up. I imagine Chains *won* this honor by being a good twenty pounds lighter than the rest of us.

He quickly realizes that the quietest way to the top, is by staying on the right side above where the supports are stabilizing the wood. Regardless, it's slow going for all of us and makes us fish in a barrel if the Bastards stop yelling at each other long enough to pay attention to their uninvited guests.

Once we're at the top of the stairs, we can hear that the argument is over demands that women be brought over to entertain them, making me relatively certain that they're focusing on each other and not the sounds of Ink breathing over my shoulder.

Chains looks at me, and at my nod, he braces his gun while he reaches up for the doorknob, which promptly comes off in his hand. The knob on the opposite side immediately falls to the floor, destroying our chance at a stealthy entrance.

"Fuck it," he says, pushing the door out and dropping to one knee. The sound of his Glock cuts through the house, with the rest of us quickly rushing in after him.

With him firing into the living room, I step directly through the opening on the other side of the hall and quickly clear what was once a kitchen, before turning in the direction of the room that Ink had indicated. A glance over my shoulder tells me that Hawk and Bishop has the same idea that I do.

The stench in the room hits us the moment I open the door. Unlike the living room and kitchen, there doesn't seem to be any working lights in here, but that's quickly remedied by the flashlight Bishop has with him.

"Connor," he whispers, his voice registers somewhere between panic and relief as a boy's bruised and bloody face is illuminated. The kid's eyes blink rapidly, momentarily blinded by the light before he lets out a muffled yell.

His body is shielding another one, their wrists and ankles seemingly bound together as they both try to wiggle enough to look at us.

It's when Alex's red, swollen eyes meet mine that I truly understand what it means to be a parent. She's safe and whole and that's all that matters to me in the entire world.

In a heartbeat, I lunge forward, pulling out my knife to slice through the zip-ties. Connor moves toward his father, and I have my arms around her, her head buried against my chest. "I got ya, sweet girl," I murmur over and over again.

She says something that I can't hear, before she slightly pushes against me. "Are you alright?" I ask, looking down at her dirt-streaked face.

"You're holding me too tight," she whispers, wiping her nose against the back of her hand. "But that's okay."

Pressing my forehead against hers, I ignore the smell of her body odor—at least I try my best to. "Did they hurt you?"

There's a world of meaning in my words and I feel her sigh. "They didn't do *that*. They said I'd be worth a lot, so the big asshole wouldn't let the others near me. They hit Connor more than they did me, barely fed us, and we could only use the bathroom once a day."

"And Connor? Is he okay?" I ask, wondering if she'll tell me something that he might not want to tell his father.

"Yeah. They kept asking him questions about the motorcycle club his dad is in. I think sometimes he'd just try to piss them off to distract them from me, though."

Maverick appears in the doorway, with Chains right behind him.

"Take the kids out of here. We got some business that needs handling, and I'm thinking it's only fair that Bishop and Silver do the honors."

"You're gonna make these fuckers pay, right?" Connor asks his dad, and I grin, instantly liking the kid.

"Already on it, son."

After hugging Alex once more, Chains wraps an

arm around her to escort her outside and I walk toward the living room. Next to the corpses, two men are being forced to kneel at gun point. One of them is shaking his head, and I'm pretty sure he's pissed himself. The one with a shaved head turns his sneer from his comrade to us, defiant as ever.

"If you kill us…"

"If?" I bark out a laugh. "You think this is a situation you're gonna walk away from?"

"Did they talk?" Bishop asks one of the Knights.

"This one has a contact," Ghost says, slapping the defiant one across the back of his head. "The kids were supposed to be passed off yesterday, but they didn't show and haven't heard anything since."

"Anything you want to add?" Bishop asks them, staring each of them down in turn.

The guy who had pissed himself opens his mouth and the other one throws his body at him. Bishop fires a round, instantly killing him.

"What were you going to say?" I ask piss-pants. His eyes say it all when he looks up at me, his face covered with his pal's blood. No matter what he tells us, he knows he's not living out the hour.

When he simply shakes his head, I reach into my boot for my knife. As Shade taught me the theory, I finally get to try cutting a man's carotid artery. Granted, I'm lucky enough to hold his head in place with my left hand as I shove the knife in next to his Adam's apple, then yank it sideways.

Fuck! I start to wipe the blade on his jeans until the flow of blood from his neck starts making more of a mess and I let the body fall before turning to wipe it on the arm of the couch.

"Shit, gimme that," Flint growls. "You go take care of your niece."

Nodding, we all file out to see that Ink has pulled his cage around and someone has wrapped blankets around the kids.

"What do we tell the cops?" Maverick asks.

Bishop and I look at each other, pausing as we stride toward Connor and Alex.

"We get the kids up the road close enough that they can walk to that gas station," Flint steps forward to lay out the plan. "They get the attendant to call one of your numbers, then wait a half an hour for you to show up."

"They don't have their phones with them," Piercer speaks up.

Somehow the look Vector gives him, doesn't drop him on the spot.

"That's the part of the plan where Bash answers our phones and rides to meet us at the gas station," Bishop picks up Flint's line of thinking. "We're so relieved that our children are physically safe that we don't call the cops until we're back home."

"There'll be a shit ton of questions," Maverick reminds us.

"Yeah, like why didn't the pigs do more to find them," Chains says, holding his hand up apologetically when Alex sucks in a deep breath. "Sorry, meant to say, 'lawyer up'."

Wrapping my arm around her, I hate the thought of being parted with her for the next part of the plan, but know it's necessary.

She looks over her shoulder to where Bishop is standing with his son. "I want to talk to him."

I nod, looking up at Bishop who seems to sense our attention, my eyes are trained on his as we start to cross the room. The moment Connor turns to look at us, Alex lets go of my hand, and continues without me, the two of them immediately join hands, and stand with barely an inch between their bodies.

I'm not more than four feet away and even that feels too far. I clench my fists, wanting to yank her back into my arms. Feeling Bishop's eyes on me, I look over at him as he crosses to join me.

"There's an app, it lets you monitor your children's texts and calls," he tells me, and I make a mental note to download it before she gets her phone back. "Connor already asked me if we can visit you sometime. Would you have a problem with that?"

"No," I try to say, but can barely get the word out as

my relief overwhelms me. "No, not at all." I forcefully push the words out this time.

"It's been a fucked-up week," he says, holding his hand out to me. "I shouldn't have said she wasn't a priority to you. One look at you together… Well, she's lucky to have you."

"I hope she thinks so one day," I reply, hating how much I like this man right now. "I'll look into that app, just as soon as I figure out how to get her to agree to one of those GPS ankle trackers."

He lets out a laugh. "Damn if I haven't wanted one on Connor since he was born."

"We're moving to Idaho as soon as we get the cops off our back for this," I let him know. "Either here or there works for a visit."

"Why don't ya come to New York?" He raises an eyebrow at me.

"Because I can barely understand you. Honestly, how do y'all have your own fucking language?" I say, laughing at him.

"You're from I-da-ho saying 'y'all', what's that about?"

"Let's get moving," Flint says, and everyone fans out to complete the plan.

SIXTEEN

SILVER

Once Bash shows up to deliver our phones, I throw a nod at Bishop but eagerly get on the road. I know Alex is exhausted, and am thankful that she's a trooper during our ride to Yanceyville's hospital.

Once the emergency room attendants see us walk in, I swear one of them are calling the cops, while the other two are trying to wrestle Alex away from me. While I hate letting her out of my sight, I decide it's the best time to call Carter.

It's either that or take the chance of getting arrested. Within thirty minutes, both Carter and the current sheriff have joined me. They ask nearly as many questions as I find on the admittance papers some administrator gave me.

Maggie practically saves the day when she and Bridget arrive.

The hospital staff was doing their best to keep me separated from my niece, at least until law enforcement had cleared me. The fact that Carter had known Maggie's grandparents his whole life, went a long way with him and he finally interceded.

"He's her legal guardian, and she's been missing for days," he insisted to Sheriff Tusco, who eventually relented, nodding to the ER nurse.

The nurse's eyes swung between me and the Northern Grizzlies who had overwhelmed the waiting room. "Only you," she said with a glare.

Maggie releases my hand, telling me to give Alex a kiss from her before going to sit down near Vector and Bridget.

"Carter, do you want to join me?" I ask him. He turns to Tusco, only getting a nod from him when one of the detectives working the case comes rushing into the hospital.

"The girl's familiar with you, so take her statement and we'll get this wrapped up," Tusco calls over his shoulder to Carter as he moves to intercept the detective.

"Doesn't seem like he cares to much about what she

has to say," I murmur as we follow the nurse past the secured doors.

"I think his accident has taken more out of him than he wants to let on. Plus, it's not like any of you or the Knights are going to give us any actual information," Carter replies, drawing out the second half of that like he'd been dropped on his head one too many times.

"I'd say my family was due a little good news, Sheriff," I say, keeping my voice firm as the nurse indicates which room to go into.

I enter ahead of him, reintroducing him to Alex.

"I want to go home tonight, Silver," she immediately says.

"I think they want to keep you here," I answer after a moment, wondering if I can disregard their advice.

"Alex, can I ask you some questions? The quicker we get through them, the sooner I'll be out of your way," Carter asks her directly, his voice taking on a kinder tone than I'm used to from him.

She nods, and is an absolute rockstar during the course of the next twenty minutes. While he does ask a few questions about why she left camp and the murder they witnessed, the rest of his questions come to a screeching halt when she says that her face was covered. Alex starts to cry, telling him the men were talking about selling her.

"You're safe now, honey," he says, putting his notepad away. He starts to reach a hand out, as though to pat her leg but stops himself. Looking at me, he tilts his head to the doorway.

"I'll do what I can to protect her from any other questions, Mr. Rawlings," he starts, speaking in a hushed tone. "May I ask if she has a therapist or anyone she can talk to?"

"We'd been seeing one in town, after her dad's death," I tell him. "But I'm moving her to Idaho with me, so I'll find someone back there as soon as I can. It definitely seemed to be a good thing for her."

"And Maggie?" he asks.

"She's coming with us," I say, finding a reason to smile. "Do you think they'd let her come back for a few minutes? I know they've gotten close."

"I'll make it happen," he assures me. "I'll be checking in on you in the coming weeks."

I'm not sure if that last part is a promise or a threat.

"Silver?" Alex calls my name as I'm watching Carter head back up the hall, stopping to talk to the nurse on duty, before he exits through the secure doors. "No more camp, okay?"

"You'll be thirty before I let you out of my sight again," I swear, turning to grin at her. The small smile she gives me tells me she thinks I'm kidding.

I'm not.

MAGGIE

Seated between Bridget and Vector, who are trying very hard to be civil to one another without addressing the major issue between them, I'm relieved when a nurse calls my name.

"Why don't y'all head to my house and get some sleep? I think we'll be fine tonight," I tell them, hoping they'll get a chance to talk, sooner than later.

I know Bridget has every intention of reaching out to Shady, at the very least. But considering how close she and Vector are, I know she wants to pick his brain some more.

Carrying the small bag filled with clean clothes for Alex, the nurse escorts me further into the hospital and my heart nearly explodes when I see her, until I notice the bruises on her arms. My nostrils flare on their own accord as I move to wrap my arms around her.

After hearing that she's physically fine, I ask Silver to go find some food for us and Alex's stomach suddenly growls.

"You know you can tell me anything, right?" I ask her. "Some things I may have to share with your uncle, but we'll discuss that before I do. I've got your back though."

"I was scared shitless, Maggie, and that was the worst of it," she tells me as tears start rolling down her cheeks. "Connor was scared too, but he hid it better than me."

"You know you had two whole motorcycle clubs looking for you? Silver forced them to put aside their differences to work to get you two back," I assure Alex. "He loves you so much."

"I knew he'd come. At least, I told myself over and over again that he would. And Connor, he would tell me all these stories about his dad. Oh! I didn't get to thank him," she says, interrupting herself.

"I'm sure, Bishop, and Miss Manners, will excuse you due to the circumstances," I sass back, getting another small smile from her. "Connor seems like a pretty good friend, huh?"

"He wouldn't have been taken if it weren't for me," she confesses, looking ashamed. "This girl was being a bitch and I decided to leave. I know I shouldn't have, but Connor guessed what I was up to and was waiting at the canoes for me."

"He definitely sounds like a good friend. I don't think any of the boys I knew at your age would have done that for me," I tell her.

"We memorized each others' numbers. We had a lot of time and it gave us something to do."

"Oh! Here," I say, reaching down for the bag I have

with me. "I brought you some clean clothes *and* your cell phone. Why don't you text him now?"

Alex eagerly reaches for the device she was forced to part with when checking into camp. "You are the best Aunt! Um, wait, are you like my aunt now, or what?"

"Well, your uncle did get around to asking me to be his Ol' Lady, so I guess I am. I hope you're alright with that?"

"He's not an idiot, of course he made you his Ol' Lady," she says with a roll of her eyes, before looking back down to send a text.

Silver rejoins us with the food that he sent someone out for, and halfway through Alex eating her and part of my order, her phone pings. The smile that lights up her face tells us both that Connor has responded.

When Silver opens his mouth, and I see the teasing look in his eyes, I glare at him. The last thing she needs right now is to be teased about having a boyfriend. Luckily, she's in her own world right now and misses that, plus how quickly his jaw snaps shut.

The next morning, we emerge to find Chains asleep in the waiting room, with Flint walking in carrying several coffees.

"I'm too damn old to sleep in those chairs," he says before turning to look at Alex. "Do you prefer pancakes or waffles? I'm hungry, how about you?"

"I like French toast," she answers after a beat.

"You know what? That sounds really good. Get it moving, Chains. I'm buying breakfast." He sounds as cranky as ever when he reaches his boot out to nudge Chains. Then he nods his head from Alex to the door and she falls into step beside him, like she's known him all her life. "I'm Flint, by the way. Are you excited about living in Idaho? Anything you want to know about Rowansville, you ask me. It's my town."

"How? What just happened?" I ask the two men I'm standing between. I've been intimidated by Flint since I met him in Idaho, not more than ten days ago. Alex just went from a kidnapping to walking away with him.

Silver starts chuckling, then Chains joins in; they share one of their looks before Silver clues me in.

"I never thought of it, but he kinda reminds me of Nathan."

Shaking my head as I make the connection, yep, I suppose she's used to straight-talking, grumpy men. God help her.

SEVENTEEN

SILVER

"What does he fucking want now?" I groan, cringing when I see the name that pops up on my caller ID.

Looking out of the back window, I can clearly see Maggie and Alex sitting on the old tree stump, chatting as the sun starts to set. While I'm relieved to have them both in my sights, part of me wishes Flint and Chains were still here.

As soon as I was heading back home with Alex, I called Carter to let him know that the kids had escaped their captors.

I exhale. Avoiding shit never solved a problem.

"Yeah?" I ask, accepting the call.

"Mr. Rawlings, I'm sure you're tired of my phone

calls," the long-winded retired sheriff starts, and that opening line does not reassure me. "I'm beginning to think you're just a manure magnet."

"Carter, as much as I appreciate your keen wit, do you mind cutting to the chase? This one time?"

"Alex's mother escaped from prison late yesterday afternoon. Sheriff Tusco is back in the office now, but I'm not sure that he should be since he didn't think to call me sooner." He pauses, possibly realizing that he went off track again. "Looks like there was a mix up and they permitted her into a low security area to meet with her attorney. From the limited information I've received, she was gone about four hours before they realized it and they don't, currently, have any leads."

"I can tell you right now, she'll be heading this way."

Fuck. I stop myself from saying anything else. That damn woman is obsessed with the idea that Nathan had a treasure trove up here. If she's on the run, she's going to want that money now more than ever. While I trust Carter to an extent, there's no way in hell I want law enforcement combing the property.

Carter promises to convince Tusco to increase patrols in the area, and to keep me up to date on any information he receives. As soon as we disconnect, I step out the back door and let out a whistle.

Now, while one of my whistles would hail any cap in New York City, Maggie and Alex barely glance in my direction. Their heads are close together and they're obviously excited about something as they continue to talk.

"Ladies?" I call out, keeping my voice even so we don't give anything away in case we're being watched. "I have a surprise for you."

In unison, they turn to look at me, then back to each other before getting up and walking back to the house. Keeping my head still, my eyes search every inch of the woods beyond them, cursing the impending darkness as I look for any hint of movement.

After Alex breezes past me, I reach for Maggie's hand and draw her up the steps. Ushering her inside, I lean closer and while she clearly expects a kiss, I whisper, "Go get your gun."

Maggie's spin immediately goes rigid, and I squeeze her hand, not wanting to spare a second.

"Alex, follow me. Stay away from the windows," I murmur, locking the door behind my niece and silently cursing myself for not getting on the road the second we recovered her.

"What's wrong?" she whispers, and my stomach churns at how pale she's turned.

"Your mother…"

"Don't call her that!" Alex had started to sit on the slab of stone that comprised the hearth, but shots back up, looking as angry as I've ever seen her.

"Prim," I say, holding my hands up in surrender.

"She's escaped from jail. Carter didn't have many details, but my best guess is that she'll head this way because she's determined to get her hands on the money she's convinced your dad had."

"About that…"

"We think we…"

Alex and Maggie speak up at the same time, then stop and exchange a smile with each other. I look between them, waiting for one of them to continue.

"The old stump, Silver," Maggie's voice is bubbling over with excitement as she continues after a nod from Alex. "When we were talking out there, I shifted over to the side because my leg was falling asleep, and the stump moved. Alex almost fell off the other side since she wasn't expecting it."

"It was strange, like it wasn't anchored into the ground by roots. I started to feel around the sides of it and the soil facing the house was really loose, while it was solidly packed in on the side facing the woods. We were just about to get up to see if we could move it when you called us to come inside!" Alex's body is nearly vibrating with excitement as she picks up the story.

"I'll be damned," I exclaim, looking between them.

"Should we go and check it out?" Maggie asks, her skin is flushed with excitement, as is Alex's. Even though adrenaline is shooting through my system, I shake my head.

"It's getting too dark, now. We're sure as shit going to keep watch tonight though," I tell them. "The last thing we need is Prim getting the drop on us, along with any of her friends."

"Let's get all packed up and ready to go," Maggie suggests. "We can put anything we want to bring with us near the front door, and handle whatever needs to be prepared for a long absence. Then we load up the truck at first light, we'll check the stump before we hightail it out of here."

"I'll have to check the woods to make sure we aren't being watched before we check it," I add on to the one point missing from her plan.

Alex immediately turns to head into her room, while Maggie does the same. I don't have much in the way of clothes, so I decide to clear out the kitchen instead. That's when it hits me, while my brother's old truck will surely get us across the country, I'd rather not take the chance if we're going to be carrying cash with us.

Pulling my cell out of my pocket, I scroll through my contacts until I find Jessup's number.

"I need a favor," I start without preamble. "I don't know how I'm going to pay you back for this, but I was wondering if you could pick me, my Ol' Lady, and niece up tomorrow?"

"Funny thing is, I'm in Georgia," he responds with a chuckle. "The judge had a heart attack and once my trial was rescheduled, I thought I'd come back and visit my brother. Text me what time you're thinking, and I'll file a flight plan. Oh, I'll need you to estimate how much your luggage will weigh. If it's too heavy, we'll have to stop to refuel along the way."

"Fucking A, man! That's great, can I let you know about the weight tomorrow? We just started packing now," I inform him. As I replay our conversation, it all clicks together in my head, and I text Flint.

I'm guessing you had a hand in Jessup's sudden visit to Georgia. Thank you.

Thank me by remembering that I hate texting.

His quick reply startles a laugh out of me before I call Roman to ask him if he's up for retrieving the truck from the airport. After a quick discussion of what to do with it, we agree on a fair price for the vehicle, and I offer to split the proceeds with him once he handles the sale.

Maggie's finished packing up our things and leaves the bags by the door, before crossing to wrap her arms around my waist. "How are you doing?"

"I want to get Alex as far away from Prim as possible. At the same time, I want to kill that bitch for what she did," I answer her as honestly as I can.

"That loose end is going to bother you, isn't it?" she asks me next, and I simply nod, heavily exhaling. "Have you, done that…killed someone before?"

Her second question comes out hesitantly, and I

wonder, not only if she wants me to answer, but what effect it will have on our relationship. I gotta roll the dice, if the shit I've done in the past—and things I might have to do in the future—is too much for her, this is the only out I'm ever going to give her.

"I have."

The words hang between us as she weighs them, waiting for me to add any details.

"Do you regret it?" Maggie keeps her face neutral, studying my eyes as she carefully asks her next question.

"Chains would be dead otherwise, so no. I've never regretted it," I honestly answer her, alluding only to one of the two men I've killed, and her blue eyes widen, surprised by that tidbit.

"Considering I'm totally in love with your godson, I'm really glad to hear that," she answers. While she tried to keep her words light and easy going, her body relaxes against mine again.

"Are you two making out? Again?" Alex asks us, sounding completely annoyed as she places two bags against the ones Maggie left near the door. "Aren't you supposed to be watching the old stump?"

"Huh," I grunt, thinking back over my conversations with my brother after her last question rang a bell in my head. "Alex, once or twice your dad said to me, 'All of my problems usually get solved out at the old stump.'."

"Yeah, he used to say that all the time," she nods her head in ready agreement. "Grandpa used to take me out there, just to sit and watch the world. He would say, 'We have everything we need, right here.', I guess I thought he meant the land would provide what we needed, but maybe they were hinting to us about the money without *actually* telling us about the money."

I tilt my head at her casual mention of my father. We'd never spoken about him, but considering he only died about six years ago, it makes sense that she'd have some memories of him. That conversation can be saved for another time—I just truly hope he was a better grandfather than he was a father.

"This is going to be the only treasure hunt we'll ever be a part of, and we have to freaking sit here all night and stare at the damn stump." Maggie nearly growls in frustration as she sums up the excitement we're all feeling.

And to her point, the night dragged on like no other night I could remember. I tossed and turned when Maggie insisted that I rest, only to have Alex tapping me on the shoulder a couple of hours before dawn. Honestly, I was impressed that she stayed awake for her shift; at least until I saw how many cans of her favorite energy drink were peeking out of the trash.

"Fuck," I whisper to myself after another hour passes. I cross to the couch where Maggie had crawled into a sleeping bag, and I gently wake her up. "Sweetheart? I'm going to scout the land a bit, I need you to lock up after me and keep an eye out."

I can't help but to smile when Maggie jumps up, as though she feels guilty for getting any sleep, and forgetting she's in a cocoon, would have fallen off of the couch if I didn't catch her.

"Sorry, sorry," she mumbles as I reach down to open the zipper on the bag.

"What for?"

"I don't know. What time is it?" Maggie's usually slow to wake up and I know the early hour isn't helping.

"It's closing in on five. I want to make the rounds a bit, then check out the stump when I'm sure the coast is clear," I speak slowly, giving her the opportunity to shake the sleep off. Nodding, she reaches into the couch cushions to retrieve her gun, checking the safety before she slides it into the pocket of the hoodie she swiped from me. "I think you might be the perfect woman."

She raises an eyebrow at me as I slowly run my eyes up and down her body, enjoying how the hoodie almost covers the shorts she's wearing, which makes her legs look extra-long. "I'm pretty sure my hair is standing on end, I haven't showered or brushed my teeth in twenty-four hours, and I'm armed. Maybe I should aim for a man with higher expectations?"

"Oh, no, you don't," I growl, reaching around her

grab a handful of her ass to pull her against me. "You're my Ol' Lady now, and I got witnesses, so no takebacks."

She dodges my mouth when I lean down to kiss her, probably nervous about her breath, and dots my collarbone and neck with light kisses while I consider dragging her to the shower for a morning romp.

"Oh my God, you two!" the resident cock-blocker shrieks as she darts from her bedroom to the bathroom.

"I love her, but I might strangle her," I grumble into Maggie's ear, getting a giggle in response.

"Go make your rounds," she says, pulling away from me. "The sooner we get out of here, the happier I'll be."

"Love you." I kiss her forehead, only stopping to point at the lock on the door, before I close it behind me.

I stay fairly close to the house, walking slowly to listen for animals and watch for any sign that someone has been trespassing. Maybe it's not the smart move, but the possibility that the old stump is hiding cash is too big of a temptation to keep me away from it any longer.

Heading to the shed, I grab the smallest shovel I can find and a crowbar before I take a moment to move my gun from the waistband of my jeans to the inner pocket of my cut.

Circling the stump, I can certainly see its appeal. Its

wide, smooth surface shows the years of hosting visitors as they'd sit to look westward through the break in the surrounding trees.

When Nathan and I were fixing up the small cabin that sits within an easy distance to the house, he told me about the storm that had cut through one summer shortly after he and our father had settled here.

This old tree had fared better than some others, but had split in half, making it entirely unsafe to leave standing. While Michael hated spending money, he hired a crew to fell it and cut the wood into boards. Considering he used those to build the shed and the additional, smaller cabin, I can only imagine how tall this tree had once stood.

Kicking at the dirt around the base of it, I understand what the girls were telling me the night before; however, it's when I push aside some of the tall grass around it, that I see what they missed. There's a latch on the side facing the house, that looks to have come loose—undoubtedly causing the wobble that sparked the girls' interest.

With a grin, I start to push at the worn wood, and nearly land on top of it when the side seemingly shoots upward. "Son of a bitch."

I catch myself against it before bending over to inspect the hood strut that I had inadvertently engaged.

"Clever bastard," are the next words out of my

mouth and I reach in to spin the dials on the combination lock. Barely hesitating, I use the four-digit code that represents Alex's birthday. Turning to look over my shoulder, I take a second to make sure I'm still alone out here.

Opening the large metal safe, I reach in to pull out a canvas bag that fits snuggly inside of it. I grossly underestimate how heavy it is, before I reach down for the other handle and use both hands and my back muscles to pull it out. Taking a deep breath, I open it and I can't help but to shake my head.

Besides the pile of cash and what looks like gold, there's the edge of an envelope peeking out.

"Don't move." It takes me a moment to realize the woman's voice is neither Maggie nor Alex and I spin on my heel, completely disobeying the command.

Whether accidentally or not, Prim fires a round that thankfully hits the stump behind me and causes Alex to scream, grabbing her ear as though she's in pain. I barely have time to register what I'm seeing, but Maggie grabs the arm holding the revolver and pushes it up with one hand while punching Prim square in the face.

Prim's nose explodes in a spray of blood, and she ends up on the ground near where her daughter is clasping her ear, her own face scrunched up in pain. From the sounds the two of them are making, there's no doubt where Alex got her voice from.

"Alex! Are you alright?" I scream, as Maggie yanks the gun from Prim's hand.

"I can't hear," my niece yells out, finally releasing her ear long enough so I can tell she's not bleeding.

"Maggie, you good?" I ask her as she holds Prim's gun on her, while I pick my niece off the ground.

"Yeah. Guess who had a spare key, by the way?" she asks, her voice tinged in annoyance. It's then that I realize that her shorts are no longer peeking out from under my hoodie and she must catch my glance because her face suddenly turns bright red. "She caught me on the toilet and wouldn't let me pull up my shorts."

I snort, shaking my head at the picture, and peek inside the house—I make sure there aren't any other unwanted guests.

"Lock the front door, then go into your room and stay there until I come and get you," I instruct Alex, speaking louder than normal since she's still holding her ear. "No games now and stay away from the window."

"Hand that to me." When I return to the women, I indicate the revolver that Prim arrived with and once Maggie hands it over, I quickly check it to make sure it's in good shape. "Where'd you park, Prim?"

"That's my money," Prim seethes, drawing her hand away from her nose and shaking the blood and snot off of it. "I earned every last dime of it, being with that asshole and having his daughter."

"Did he get it from his dad?"

She shrugs when I ask that. "I guess so. Nathan always acted like he was scraping by, so I don't really know nothing. Just the rumors I heard about Michael, and there's no way that mean old bastard got it legally."

The acid in my stomach kicks up a notch and I spit on the ground near her feet. It makes me sick, thinking of the years I went to bed hungry while my old man was sitting on a pile of cash. Not that he ever bothered to track me down.

"Get up," I tell her, and feeling Maggie's hand on my back, I indicate the bag to her. "Would you mind keeping an eye on that for me, babe?"

She fishes her own gun out of the hoodie's pocket and murmurs her agreement.

"I ain't going back to jail," Prim says, her eyes taking on a wild look.

"No, Prim, you aren't going back to jail," I agree with her, before I point to the path I want her to take. "Walk down that way."

"My car's the other way," she wails.

"You won't be needing your car, Prim," I tell her, just as calm as can be.

"How do you think Alex is going to live with you, knowing that you killed her mother?" she taunts me, backing in the opposite direction from where I told her to go.

"Peacefully," I answer her, getting tired of her attempts to stall this. "We talked last night. She didn't even shed a tear. And me? I'll just be happy not to have to be looking over my shoulder for you the rest of my life."

With those words, she charges at me, a pen knife suddenly flashing in her hand, and I shoot her right shoulder, spinning her around as the small knife goes flying. Her screams seem louder than the echo of the gunshot, and I step toward her, wishing she had at least moved in the direction of the cliff where I had every intention of ending her life.

Coming up behind her as she tries to crawl away, I grab her by the back of her neck to drag her toward the ravine where I had planned on tossing her body.

"You killed my brother. Slow and hard. Now, it's your turn."

Her pleas for mercy fall on deaf ears. I am not that type of man.

After firing the next round into her stomach, I shove her body over the edge, into the deep ravine. The only thought I have as I lean down to pick up the bullet casing is that maybe, just maybe, I have more of my father in me than I had considered.

Tossing the casing up into the air, I catch it and slide it into my pocket. A morbid reminder of justice served.

I carefully trudge back to the cabin, keeping my eyes on the ground for any sign of her footprints or of blood that might have fallen from her initial wound. Stopping just before the clearing, I see that Maggie has hefted the bag on top of the stump and is peeking inside of it.

"He wrote you a letter," she says before I can say anything. She holds the envelope out in my direction until I step forward for it. "There are jewels in here, too. Not just cash. I assume they're real, but it's not like I'd know the difference."

"Would you mind going to check on Alex for me?" I ask her, clearing my throat when I barely recognize my own voice.

"Are you alright?" she quietly asks me, and it isn't the first time I wonder how in God's name I got so lucky.

"Yeah, I'm just going to read it out here," I tell her, taking it after I move the bag and sit on the old stump.

Maggie reaches out, running her hand through my hair and kissing my forehead, before heading back to the house.

I pull the letter out, and my heart starts beating harder and harder when I see the necklace that's tucked inside of it.

Sam,

This money is as much yours as it was mine. I can't tell you how our father got it, and honestly,

I think it's better that we don't know.

I'd ask that you split it with my baby girl. Please do right by her, and always make sure she

knows that I loved her more than anything on this planet.

When he died, I found Mom's necklace among Michael's things. I don't know if you remember,

but I knew it immediately. Mom never took it off and I am certain she was wearing it the day we drove away from you two.

I remembered it better than I did her face, at least until you showed up. Your features and expressions have brought back so many memories of her. At the time I found it, I just shrugged, having long thought she was dead anyway. Since you came, well, I still think the same, and again, have no answers for you.

You'll never know how grateful I am that your stubborn ass spent years looking for me.

I am glad we got the chance to be brothers again.

Nathan

Taking a moment, I carefully fold the letter and put in the inside pocket of my cut. I put the necklace around my neck, then heft the bag into both arms before joining the girls. For the first time in my life, the future doesn't worry me.

How could it? With Maggie by my side and Alex back safe and sound.

Looking over my shoulder one last time, I nod in the direction of the stump—making a silent promise to my brother that his daughter will be loved and safe.

EPILOGUE

SILVER

IDAHO, THREE YEARS LATER

After looking down at my wife's sleeping form, I tip toe out of the room, barely able to comprehend how we've gotten to this place.

When I make sure the door closes without so much as a whisper of noise, Chains catches my eyes and I hold my hand up to place a finger over my lips.

"Shit," he mumbles, chuckling as he leads the way up the hall. "You're making me feel like we're in junior high again!"

"We missed toasting your daughter's birth, so we'll toast her and Caroline now," I remind him, opening the door to the stairwell that heads up to the roof of Rowansville's only hospital. Most of us have been up here at some point, blowing off steam while waiting on the outcome of surgeries or births. An occasional death, but I'm too fucking happy to think about those now.

Sitting on the edge of the building, he puts the pints of Jack between us and hands me a cigar. We both light 'em up before we crack open our bottles.

"Having the insight of raising a teenage girl, I can't imagine this will be too hard," I say and Chains bursts out laughing. Maggie and I love Alex dearly, but that girl has been a handful. If not for the college entrance exams taking place tomorrow, she'd have been camped out at the hospital during Maggie's short labor.

"To fatherhood," Chains says, clinking his bottle against mine. "May we do better than those before us."

Repeating the pledge he made when his son was born, this time to include me, I repeat his words to myself.

"Having the insight of raising a teenage girl, at least I know what to expect," I say and Chains bursts out laughing. Maggie and I love Alex dearly, but that girl has been a handful. If not for the college entrance exams taking place tomorrow, she'd have been camped out at the hospital during Maggie's short labor.

Even though I'm just a floor up from Maggie and our daughter, it's the furthest I've been from them in the six hours since Caroline was born, and I find myself worried that Maggie won't see the note I left her if she wakes up.

I hope she knows, I can't imagine any scenario where I'd ever walk away from them. Maggie has helped me make peace with the fact that I'll never know why my father didn't try to find me. And was surprisingly understanding when we talked about looking into what happened to my mother.

Fred's words from our first meeting have often rung in my head, and as bat-shit crazy as he and his wife can act sometimes, they danced front and center when I decided to count the blessings that I had rather than chasing what I didn't.

For a kid with nothing but a string of failed foster and group homes behind me, I could now count my niece, Maggie, our first born, the Dennisons, and Chains's family as my own. Not to mention the Northern Grizzlies.

My family.

Taking another swig from the bottle, I stand up and howl like a maniac at the moon. Instead of laughing at me, Chains does the same and it's like we're ten years old all over again.

"I think it was Bree who once repeated a quote from some book she had read," he says, after blowing a few smoke rings into the cool night air. "It was after I had met Soph, so it really stood out in my head. 'Some people are born into their families, and others have to find theirs.'. That's us, brother. That's us, and I wouldn't have it any other way."

"Amen," I reply, except when I hold up my bottle for the last sip, I'm thinking of Nathan and wishing he was still with us.

"Yeah. Him too." Chains claps me on my back as I'm checking the time on my phone. "Now, get your ass downstairs before Mags wakes up."

Sneaking back into Maggie's room, I check on our daughter before lowering myself into the chair next to her bed.

"Did you save any for me?" Her question startles a laugh out of me.

"The cigar or the whiskey?"

"Asshole," she chuckles.

"I promise, just as soon as you're cleared, we'll get Chains and Sophia to take Alex and Caroline for an overnight," I tell her, picking up her hand to kiss it. "We'll get a hotel room, a fancy-as-fuck steak dinner, and even go dancing, if that's what you want. Actually, we'll make it two nights, so you can recover from the first. How does that sound?"

"That sounds like our second child will be along next year." Maggie's smile pulls at my heart.

I can easily see how tired she is, but her love shines clearly in her eyes when I lean forward to kiss her. Just then her phone pings, and my eyes shift to the screen.

"Oh, God," she whispers, clearly reading the expression on my face. "When will they be here?"

"Two days," I answer, pinching the bridge of my nose between my fingers.

Just then our daughter starts to fuss, and I pick her up as carefully as anyone would handle an unstable stick of dynamite. Transferring her to Maggie's arms, I remember her exact reasons for us eloping to Vegas, just as she opens her mouth to speak.

"Do you think the Northern Grizzlies are ready for Grandma?" Maggie asks with a crooked grin on her face, freeing a nipple before she awkwardly tries to coax our baby to nurse.

"I knew she'd be coming, and *I'm* still not ready for her," I answer, shaking my head with a matching grin on my face. "But, fuck, it'll be fun to watch her unveil her particular brand of crazy on them."

A NOTE FROM MERIN

Well – this book was never planned,

but SO much fun to write and put together with Janine's *Cross to Bear*!

Thank y'all for sticking with me and my imaginary friends. There aren't words to express my gratitude about how you've received the Northern Grizzlies, ever since I stumbled onto the Indie scene in 2018.

And this ride isn't over yet!

As I've mentioned in various posts, the Next Generation books are underway – kicking off with Gunner's very determined daughter.

(Hmm, where does she get that from?)

And yes, I think that the Virginia NGMC stories need to be told.

XO, Merin

MORE BOOKS BY M. MERIN

Northern Grizzlies MC Series:

Jasper (Book 1)

Flint (Book 2)

Gunner (Book 3)

Charlie (Book 4)

Michaels (Book 5)

Betsy (Book 6)

Shade (Book 7)

Royce (Book 8)

Silver's Bullet (Book 9)

Chains: Northern Grizzlies MC Short I

Wrench: Northern Grizzlies MC Short II

Royal Bastards MC, Flagstaff Chapter:

Axel (Book 1)

Declan (Book 2)

Diesel (Book 3)

Snowed In: A Royal Bastard Surprise (Book 4)

Wolfman (Book 5)

Throttle (Book 6)

Big Timber – 2024

The Grave Knights MC:

Me'ansome (Book 1)

Tin (Book 2)

Ever After

Dark Ever After (Book 1)

Julia's Journey (Book 2)

Defending Our Ever After (Book 3)

Book 4 - Not yet named

Also Available

Black Hills Shifters Books 2 & 4

His Touch

Molotov Brothers: The Reluctant King (Book 1)

Kal: A Rogue Enforcers Novella

The Weight of Blood

ABOUT M. MERIN

Merin was raised in the Midwest but has drifted across the country, unconsciously collecting stories from the world around her.

A wife, an avid reader, a doting dog-mama and aunt. She loves classic rock & country music and ice hockey – preferably the Blackhawks, but nowadays she can be found at Griffin's games.

Made in the USA
Middletown, DE
14 March 2024

51516870R00136